The GREATEST STORY UNTOLD

www.parislovesall.com

Paperback ISBN: 978-1-63616-055-9
eBook ISBN: 978-1-63616-056-6

Published By Opportune Independent Publishing Co.
www. opportunepublishing.com

Printed in the United States of America
For permission requests, email the author with the subject line as "Attention: Permissions Coordinator" to the email address below:

Info@opportunepublishing.com
www. opportunepublishing.com

First, I have to give all thanks and praise to my creator and my ancestors for giving me the strength, wisdom and knowledge to share and create a story that my readers will enjoy.

I could not have created such a great masterpiece without the support of my friends and family. The journey was long and hard. I now have a higher level of respect for authors than before because this process is not an easy one… However, this is my first book but not my last. This book is my baby and it was a very tedious task nurturing it. This has been one of the most difficult projects that I've ever worked on but the love and support of others kept me going even when I was ready to throw in the towel. I would have never thought or imagined at 32 years old that I would've become an author. I surely didn't think that I would have a physical book in my hands that I wrote. I hope you guys enjoy the read!

I want to thank the love of my life, Andre, for pushing me to complete my book with tough love. It would've never happened otherwise. His tender love and care are the reasons that this beautiful garden has flourished. His exact words were, "Babe, I see this becoming a movie. I believe this will happen one day." Thank you so much for your time, patience and love.

I want to thank one of my biggest supporters, Chatfield J. Sr., author of Death After Betrayal. During the making of this book, he gave me his feedback and how he felt about certain scenes. I remember at one point after reading something he would say, "You can do better than that." That kind of inspiration pushed me even harder and it was truly a blessing. He was actually one of the first people who read my book in its entirety and it inspired him to write his own great masterpiece.

I want to thank Miss Johnson for listening to me read as I wrote and edited my book. She always gave her love, support and honest opinion. She also challenged my creativity and writing abilities which kept me going. It was like turning your essay into your college professor to grade it. Thank you for the Love and support.

Thank you to my sister, La'Quanna Howard, who also pushed me and believed in me even when I didn't believe in myself.

I want to give a big thanks to Just'n Francois, who is one of the characters inside the book. His influence, spiritual guidance and love challenged me to take my book to the next level. Thank you so much. Check out his skincare line www.facebyfrancois.com

I want to give a special thanks to another one of my supporter who was there before I started writing and at the birth of my book. I was just working on the book cover and trying to figure out what I wanted to write, and he sat there for countless hours and listened to the many ideas I had. He then helped me come up with a title that turned into The Greatest Story Untold. Thank you so much Errol Moore.

I want to say thank you to Deverist Daughtry for Inspiring me to reach for the stars and work hard to make all my dreams come true.

I have to give thanks to Tokyo for believing in me. Tokyo pushed me and was so super excited when I started this journey. Thank you so much, my love and I love you with all my heart.

Support comes in many shapes and forms. Monae' Mullannii Whitfield was the many shapes and forms when I was feeling discouraged, he kept me laughing and fueled my creativity. Thank you so much.

Thanks, Mom and Dad for all the love and support that you've provided. Can't forget about my second Mom, Adrian Reese, for giving me the right amount of love, peace, knowledge and wisdom.

I could never forget about the one and only Legend, one of my first editors who also enhanced my writing abilities, his special touch played a major role and influence. He helped me become a better author and a better version of myself. He poured so much knowledge and wisdom into me and the wisdom he gave me turned into pages and pages of entertainment that you the reader can enjoy. Love you bunches Walter Dawson AKA Legend.

Thank you to Shanley McCray for believing in my craft. She was so excited about my project which pushed me even harder to get this project moving. She was the first professional publishing company that got their hands on my book and her support was like no other. I had speculations that I had a great masterpiece but Mrs. McCray and Opportune Independent Publishing Co. confirmed the many years of hard work that I put into this project. During the major editing of this book, the editors at Opportune Independent Publishing Co. and I were like peanut butter and jelly; ketchup and mustard on hamburgers and hotdogs; cereal and milk. Thank you Shanley

McCray, for believing in me and turning my work into an even greater masterpiece.

Thank you to all my supporters, peace, love and blessing to all.

Current Mood: Elevated
The Song: Celia Song by Artist Tiwa Savage

DEDICATION

Let me first warn you that what you are about to read can become a good addiction or a bad addiction. This story has never been told, so watch it unfold. I am going to walk with you patiently and gently, hold your hand, as I walk you through the four corners of the Earth. We will hover the land, and together, we will reign for eternity. This is not a myth, but a reality that has value as well as honesty. Be open-minded and be careful with your steps. Forward, there's nothing… if there is no understanding. The future is everything, but so is the past if properly nurtured. We're going on a roller coaster ride to the seventh dimension, the eighth dimension, the twelfth dimension and all the way to the twentieth dimension. Together, we will swim to the deepest, darkest oceans that man has never apprehended before. Also, we will explore the twelve levels of the belly of the beast. This will give you clarification on what you have read and what you are about to read. Be extra careful, because Charlotte's web is attached. You might get tangled in it—and there is no way to escape her venom.

Remember, knowledge is power, yet what is power if there is nobody to have power over? So, the real question becomes, ''Who's playing the puppet-master and who is the puppet?''

If you're scared, then hang in there and cling tightly to my hand, as I've warned you. May the Most High One's love, protection and blessings be upon all my readers who embrace the hidden knowledge within this great book. Now, follow me and enjoy the greatest story as it unfolds.'

Written by: Paris D
07/2021

CONTENTS

CHAPTER 1
MAN + BEAST = "GOD"

It was mild and cold on this January morning. It was the year 2012; everything seemed to be falling apart for Zeke. It didn't matter what, how, when or where things assumed to be, it… just wasn't right for him.

You see, the young man had been floating for a long time, making his money his debut as well as his friends'. He enjoyed the fame and the fast cash, but life at home wasn't truly a life at home. Could Zeke really survive his own mistake, or would his past catch up to him and kill him? Or, would it lead him to hurt the women of his dreams? It's true of the celebrities he once met and the cars he once drove, but the alpha and omega are inevitable. His disposition has its own entourage of demons, lies and murder. This was a point in time when the young man was about to do whatever it took to become successful.

ONE MONTH LATER:

"Bartender! Another, please!" Zeke asked while sipping on a half-finished Red Bull.

So this is my life? Zeke asked himself. His thoughts were suddenly interpreted as the bartender approached him with a welcoming smile. "Here you go, babe. Can I get you anything else?" the bartender asked.

"Make it a double," Zeke demanded while throwing back his fourth shot.

"Would you like a glass of water?" Tina asked as she looked at him with her seductive brown eyes.

Tina was about five feet, four inches tall, and her beautiful chocolate skin looked like soft silk. Her Jamaican accent made her extra spicy. Her hair was pulled into a nice ponytail and the baby hairs on her forehead were partly laid. Anyone would notice that she had been working, as her nails were slightly chipped and her eyebrows needed to be waxed. The stains on her shoes matched the stains on her jeans. As Tina mixed Zeke's drinks, he admired her natural curves. As Tina worked the bar, Zeke continued to admire her Jamaican genetic makeup; she had thick thunder thighs that jiggled to the beat of each and every step she took. Her perfectly round ass followed suit; it was as if her body had its own natural rhythm.

Zeke got aroused as he watched her work the crowd.

Maybe I should slow down on the shots, because this island girl got me hypnotized, Zeke thought to himself.

"Heeeey! Snap out of it!" Tina yelled with a welcoming smile.

Her teeth were whiter than the clouds in the sky.

"Thanks for the water. Has anybody ever told you that you have beautiful teeth?" Zeke asked while taking a sip of the water Tina just gave him. Zeke sipped on the ice cold water. It was quite refreshing. Each and every sip he took hydrated his mind, body and soul.

"Don't be flirting with me, man. I'm here to do my job," Tina said very playfully in her strong Jamaican accent. "If you need anything else, let me know," said Tina, while helping a drunk couple next to Zeke.

While reggae music filled the speakers inside the small bar, Zeke watched Tina roll her hips very seductively to the rhythm. She didn't miss a beat; the way she rotated her hips, you knew that the girl had skills. As Tina continued dancing, she looked Zeke in his brown eyes.

She continued giving him the eye because she knew he was tipsy and slick choosing. I know that he's gonna leave me a fat tip. If I wasn't at work, I would've rode him right here on the dance floor, thought the determined, underpaid bartender.

RIIIINNNNNNGGGG! RRRRRRIIINNNNGGG!

Zeke's dirty drunk thoughts were quickly interrupted by the sounds of his device. He quickly reached inside the pockets of his all-white designer jeans that cost more than a stack. Zeke was light skinned with a perfectly trimmed goatee He stood at five feet, nine inches with a pair of hazel brown eyes that were so captivating and electrifying that he could turn Medusa into stone. Zeke always demanded attention when he stepped into any room. There was no doubt that Zeke was a boss and a sex symbol. Once he pulled the device out of his front right pocket, he Looked down at the screen. It read, Incoming call from Dream.

Zeke immediately pressed the answer button.

"What's up, Dream?" Zeke said in a very dry tone.

"What the hell is wrong with you, fool?" Dreamed asked.

"Nothing much," Zeke lied.

"Something is wrong! Don't shoot me no BS. You think I

don't know when something is bothering you? I've been knowing you before you started knowing yourself! Now, what's wrong?" Dream said in a very demanding/concerned tone of voice.

"It's Autumn," Zeke said while signaling Tina the bartender to bring another round of Patrón shots.

"What's going on with y'all now? I will push that trick on her knees if she hurt you!" Dream said with lots of enthusiasm.

"No need. We broke up," Zeke said.

"Oh, I'm sorry to hear that, man. That's why you're taking shots like a madman," said Tina while handing Zeke his seventh shot.

"Who the hell is that?" Dream asked.

"That's the bartender," Zeke replied

"Tell her to mind her own damn business before she ends up on a T-shirt!" Dream yelled into the phone.

"Dream, leave her alone. She's keeping me company," Zeke replied with lots of seduction within his voice.

"What bar are you currently located at?" Dream asked.

"I'll send you the address," Zeke replied.

"Hurry up and send the location, because you are not going home tonight with a thirsty bartender who has a pair of stained jeans and shoes," said Dream while grabbing her car keys off the kitchen counter.

"Dream, don't be rude," replied Zeke while checking Tina out once again.

Am I drunk, or does Tina make a pair of stained jeans look good? Zeke thought to himself while listening to Dream enter her BMW X5.

"OK, Zeke. See you in about 15 minutes," Dream said, then

ended the call.

Ring! Ring! Ring!

Zeke's phone rang right after he disconnected from Dream. Damn, I'm booming! He thought to himself before answering his phone.

"Hello?" Zeke answered.

"Hey, are you OK?" Autumn asked with concern in her voice.

Should I hang up? Zeke asked himself before he responded.

"I'm at a bar," replied Zeke.

"A bar?" Autumn asked with lots of disappointment in her voice.

"So, is this your new life? Getting drunk and shit, that ain't gon' solve nothing," Autumn said.

It's just… never mind," Zeke said while devouring another shot.

"Do you even miss me?" Autumn asked.

"I do," Zeke replied.

"What happened to us?" Autumn asked.

"There's lots of shit going on. We got these crazy ass people on our backs," she said with a concerned heart. "Have you even come up with a plan?" Autumn asked.

"No, I haven't come up with a plan, but maybe we should meet once I leave this place," Zeke suggested.

"OK. I would love that," Autumn said.

15 MINUTES LATER:

Zeke continued to fill his belly with Patrón shots, and each shot he took impaired him even more. His reflexes and response time were even compromised. Usually, Zeke would sense someone's spirit entering his aura, but in this present moment, he didn't realize that someone was behind him... "Where's my shot!?" yelled Dream.

"Come on, Dream! Please have a seat. You can't just sneak up on me like that," Zeke said while taking his hand off his nine-millimeter that was sitting perfectly inside his gun holster.

Zeke quickly signaled Tina to bring him and Dream another round of shots. Four shots later, Tina came over and her demeanor had completely changed. "I think you guys have had enough for tonight," Tina said while rolling her eyes at Dream.

Dream flashed Tina a quick smile and said, "Nobody asked you if we had enough to drink. Awww, she's jealous. Girl... you don't have to worry about me. Zeke is family. You know what? I was gonna leave you a big enough tip so that your busted ass could get a new uniform. Matter of fact, I will leave that tip! So, you can treat yourself to a pedicure, and I'm pretty sure those dusty ass eyelashes need to be replaced, too. Here's an extra $50 so you can also get them overdue and overgrown ass eyebrows waxed," Dreamed said while throwing $300 in Tina's face.

"Zeke, you gotta be drunk!" Dream said as she finished her drink.

"She is a ratchet ass bartender," Dream said with lots of venom in her tone.

"Can you close my tab?" Zeke asked Tina while attempting to keep Dream calm.

"We've had enough to drink! Ha!" Dream chuckled after embarrassing Tina.

At that present moment, Tina knew the best thing she could do was just walk away. While closing out Zeke's tab, Tina felt a sense of guilt. Unable to look Zeke in the eyes, she handed him his debit card. Zeke quickly handed her the same $300 that Dream had just thrown in her face. Before Zeke left the bar, he slid her an additional $300 for her troubles. Tina then watched Zeke in disbelief as he disappeared through the crowd.

"Zeke, you tripping… was you planning on having sex with her?" Dreamed asked with a sarcastic smile.

"I wasn't," Zeke replied.

"So, what's up with you and Autumn?" Dream asked.

"She wants to meet tonight," Zeke replied while checking to see if he had any missed calls.

"Are you ready for that?" asked Dream.

"I'm always ready," Zeke replied with a slur in his voice.

"OK. Do you need me to go with you? Just in case I gotta pull her weave out?" Dream asked.

"No, Dream. No violence tonight," Zeke replied while showing Dream the location to drive to.

"Zeke! Just be careful, and if you need me, I'm here."

"Thanks, D, for having my back," Zeke said, with his eyes closed and his head on the headrest of Dream's X5.

25 MINUTES LATER:
Autumn's House

When Autumn opened the front door to her house, Zeke had almost forgotten how incredibly beautiful she was. Zeke quickly dismissed the thoughts and walked past her. He needed to sit down because the amount of alcohol that he consumed had him buzzing.

"Wow, that was rude of you," said Autumn while following him into the living room.

"Sit down! Don't you wanna talk?" Zeke asked while making himself a little bit more at home.

Damn! He looks good, Autumn thought to herself.

"How have you been, baby?" Zeke Asked, with a grin.

"Don't 'baby' me," Autumn said while fighting temptations.

"You shouldn't act like that. I still love you and I know you still love me," she said.

The more time they spent in each other's presence, the flames that once burned began to ignite. When they moved a little closer, the flames within them burned brighter and brighter! The love that they shared couldn't never truly die, so it allowed them to break the invisible barrier that was standing between them. Once Autumn let her guards down, she began to vent about why she felt that the love and trust within their relationship was broken.

"I thought you were gonna turn against me," Autumn said with lots of pain in her voice.

"Why would you think that?" Zeke asked with a sudden look of confusion.

"Your vibes made me feel like you were switching up on me," she said while rolling her eyes.

"I would never betray you, Autumn," Zeke said as he kissed Autumn on the lips very passionately.

Zeke's soft, gentle and wet kisses sent instant chills throughout Autumn's entire body. "Zeke!" she moaned softly.

While holding each other throughout the night, Zeke and Autumn decided to come up with a master plan to destroy the two gentlemen who wanted to destroy them.

"Zeke!" Autumn whispered softly as she lay on his chest peacefully.

"Yes, Autumn?" Zeke Asked.

"We never finished the job," Autumn said, this time with a hit of concern within her voice.

"What job?" Zeke asked as he held Autumn closer to him.

"I'm gonna say one word, and the word is 'Yasmeen,'" Autumn replied very softly.

Oh, shit… I totally forgot, Zeke thought to himself.

Ring! Ring! Ring!

"Hello?!" Zeke Answered.

"WHAT THE HELL?! HAPPENED TO YOU?!" Yasmeen screamed.

"Something came up and I had to…" before Zeke could utter another word, Yasmeen quickly interrupted.

"I DON'T WANT TO HEAR YOUR SORRY EXCUSES!" Yasmeen yelled in a strong Tehran accent.

"Listen, Yasmeen. During the job that Mr. Henderson hired us to do, somebody tried to kill one of my family members. I believe the whole entire mission was set up," Zeke said while he continued to caress Autumn.

"Zeke, if what you're saying is true, this is madness. Madness, I tell you. Mr. Henderson has already put a hit out on you and Autumn. He told me to tell you that he's going to make you disappear completely," Yasmeen said very coldly.

Yasmeen was the most beautiful exotic Persian hired hit-woman anyone had ever seen. Her beauty was her venom. To the naked eye, she appeared as a rich, powerful princess who lived in a palace somewhere in Abu Dhabi. Standing at five feet, seven inches, she had a very petite body frame. Her soft, smooth milk-and-honey skin had a natural glow to it. This complemented her exotic features, making her appear as a goddess. Yasmeen had told Zeke that before she murdered someone, she would make the individual stare into her beautiful green eyes. It was said that she captured the souls of the unlucky prospects who crossed her path. This is one black mamba whose path you didn't want to cross.

"Yasmeen! I would like you to relay a personal message to Mr. Henderson for me," Zeke said in a very cocky tone.

"I'm not getting involved in this," Yasmeen replied, and this time, her accent was very strong.

"You're already involved," Zeke said very coldly.

"Choose your words wisely. If I sense any form of disrespect from you, I will put one slug into your forehead and another into Autumn. Hahaha, how sweet. You two will die holding each other," Yasmeen said with no remorse.

"Holy shit… Yasmeen is outside the house," Zeke informed Autumn while using telepathic waves.

Autumn instantly jumped up, but Zeke quickly apprehended her.

"Listen, Yasmeen. There's no beef or bad blood between us. I just want you to get a quick message to Mr. Henderson," Zeke said very calmly.

"Oh! Now you speak with sense. I see you took the aggression out of your voice," Yasmeen said as she aimed an infrared light directly at Zeke's temple.

"Now, talk! And if you make this message too long, I'm going to send you and your girlfriend to meet your creator. Tick, tock… You may speak now!" Yasmeen said as she took control of the entire situation.

"Let Mr. Henderson know that my father, Mr. Banks, is well connected. Also inform him that he doesn't want the kind of problems that I will bring," Zeke said as he watched the infrared beam disappear.

"TTYL! Zeke, if you're ever in my country, you have my math," Yasmeen said as she discontinued the telephone call.

"What the hell is going on?" Autumn asked in concern.

"Don't worry. It's all going to be over soon," Zeke replied with murder in his heart.

7:07 a.m.:

Beep! Beep!

Zeke was awoken by the sounds of his cellular device going mayhem. He quickly reached for his phone that laid on the nightstand next to him. Autumn quickly grabbed his hand to assure that everything was fine.

"Everything is OK," Zeke said to Autumn while using telepathic waves. Autumn immediately nodded her head and laid back down. When Zeke opened his phone, there was a text message from an unfamiliar number.

The mysterious text message read:

Good morning! We got off on the wrong foot. I don't want you to worry about the unfinished job assignment that you didn't complete. Just to prove to you that there is no bad blood between us, I'm sending you and another person of your choice on an all-expenses-paid trip to London. The tickets will be sent to you via email.

Safe travels.

— Mr. Henderson

That was random, Zeke thought to himself in disbelief.

Mr. Henderson, what do you have up your sleeve? You're not the type of man who surrenders nor retreats? Something doesn't feel right, Zeke thought in suspicion while showing Autumn the message that was just sent to him.

"I don't trust it. Zeke, it's a set up," Autumn said with lots of passion.

"I agree with you!" Zeke replied with vengeance in his heart.

Mr. Henderson thinks he's the only one who knows how to play a good game of chess, he thought to himself while letting out a slight chuckle.

The following morning, Mr. Henderson received a big, mysterious box that was delivered to his doorstep. The box contained certain items and information that was tied to his mama. **Items inside the mysterious box were labeled as followed:**

(1) SAID ITEM NUMBER ONE: HER CHURCH WIG.

(She has been wearing this wig every Sunday since Mr. Henderson was a child. We also know what church she attends. I'm aware that by now, you're wondering who this is. Just know that the little church by the elementary school on Askew Lane down from the Penny Man's Store is where your mother goes to church service every Sunday. She has been devoted since you were a child.

Once reading the notes attached to the items inside the

mysterious box, Mr. Henderson immediately panicked and started to wonder who this person is and what type of connections they have.

(2) SAID ITEM NUMBER TWO: HER MEDICATION BAG

Mr. Henderson was very confused and wondered how they got to his mother's meds. At that time, he thought to himself, *It's time to give Mama her meds.* He continued to read the attached small note, which read:

By now, it should have already sunk through your thick, inconsiderate brain that this isn't any kind of hoax. We will poison her with no regrets. Life has meaning just as well as precision; therefore; your decision has been chosen, and Mama can pay the price… isn't that how it goes?

(3) SAID ITEM NUMBER THREE: A COPY OF HER CAR KEY.

(We will blow Mama's ass to the moon and won't lose a single breath of air or any sleep. When you play with the game, then respect the repercussions that come with it.)

(4) SAID ITEM NUMBER FOUR: THE ORIGINAL COPY OF HER UTILITY BILL

By now, Mr. Henderson paced through his 24-room luxurious estate, while sweat ran down his face and rage and fear trampled his heart. He couldn›t stop now, 'cause he required more information; therefore, he continued his search by reading on. What he discovered in the final briefing stunned the old fellow. The note read as follows:

Mr. Henderson, you might not want to have a heart attack right now. Instead, you might want to sit down and breathe slowly, 'cause if you die on me, then who's going to protect Mama? This could be a peace treaty or your mother's death certificate. The next decision that you make decides your mother's life. It will determine whether anthrax will be delivered to her mailbox or not. Don't try to play me, either, 'cause the question remains... When will her anthrax be delivered? It could be today or tomorrow... Oh, yeah, by the way.. .isn't she on her way at this very moment to her mailbox to pick her mail up?

The note ended, but not Mr. Henderson, 'cause he knew that somewhere, someone was watching, and they were doing a damn good job on their homework...

We will murder Mama, so stand down, read the small tag on the big red box)

GOD IS LOVE

CHAPTER 2
THE TRANSFORMATION

15 MINUTES LATER:

"He hasn't said a word," Autumn said as she paced back and forth inside a small, run-down Motel room. "Does this mean we won? she asked.

"You can never be too sure, dealing with guys like him," Zeke said as sweat dripped from his face.

The air conditioning had stopped working inside the cheap room they were in a day ago.

"They're trying to kill us slowly! He's here... he clipped the wires to the A/C unit! They are trying to suffocate us to make us come out of the room!" Autumn said as she continued panicking.

The summer heat was frying her brain.

"That's not his style," Zeke said while trying to keep his sanity.

"How do you know what his style is?" Autumn asked with desperation in her voice.

"Don't panic. I have a plan," Zeke said while grabbing Autumn's hand. "We leave at sundown and whatever happens, happens. The longer we stay in this room, the more we are putting ourselves at risk of a heat stroke."

Zeke quickly ran to the bathroom and ran cold water onto a

rag. He then placed it on Autumn's forehead while she laid on the uncomfortable and itchy bed.

"I hope we make it out of here alive," Autumn whispered as the rag cooled her down.

Zeke tried to come up with a sensible escape plan, but nightfall came quicker than he thought.

"Autumn, call the front desk and make some type of scene," Zeke said while peeking out the window.

"That's your master plan?" she asked while picking up the old motel phone.

"Front desk," said the receptionist.

"Can you send maintenance to room 303? Also, I need to tell you something in private. I can't make it to the front desk, if you know what I mean."

"Oh! Of course. We will be right up," the lady replied.

"Zeke, grab the other lamp," Autumn instructed.

Zeke quickly followed suit because he knew exactly what was about to go down.

Knock, knock!

"It's hotel personnel," Autumn said. She quickly opened the door.

As the two clueless motel workers walked in the room, they said, "Oh, looks like there's a power outage!" A sudden blow to the head with the lamp dropped the maintenance man to the floor, and Autumn hit the old lady over the head with the other cheap motel lamp. Zeke quickly checked for a pulse.

"They're very much alive!" Zeke said, using telepathic waves to survey the situation.

Autumn took the lady's uniform and placed her on the bed;

Zeke followed suit. While Autumn changed, Zeke staged the room. He made it look as if the both of them were having an affair on the job.

They're gonna get fired, Autumn thought as they escaped into the night.

The mysterious box the pair had delivered to Mr. Henderson's doorstep was a declaration of war. The both of them knew that there would be consequences and repercussions. None of that really mattered though; they were still alive, and that's all that mattered in the present moment. Zeke and Autumn made one of the most dangerous men in the world back down—they had just made history. The real question became, How long do they have to live? The two of them needed to come up with a plan, and *fast*. Both of them knew that their lives would never be the same again.

"Zeke, I'm done hiding in the shadows!" Autumn cried. "If he touches one of us, I'ma murder his mama my damn self," she yelled with war in her voice.

"I need you to go off the grid completely until we figure this out," Zeke said in hopes that she would understand.

Autumn looked deeply into Zeke's eyes and searched for some kind of hidden agenda or motive. She was waiting for a smile, or for a camera crew to jump out of the woods and tell her she was being punk'd, but none of those things came true.

"What will you do?" Autumn asked, worried.

"I have to keep my eyes and ears in the streets," Zeke said while booking a private jet for Autumn's departure.

"Zeke, cancel the jet. I have to utilize my own resources. Everything has to be untraceable. Clearly, you were just about to leave a paper trail. I know a place that's super safe and private. It's totally exclusive; it's not even marked on the world map! When I arrive, there will be no way for you to contact me," Autumn said as she took control of her life.

Autumn knew that the decision they just made would be hard, but it was for her own safety. She hugged and kissed Zeke like it was the last time she ever would. Autumn quickly disappeared without a trace while Zeke hid in the one place Mr. Henderson would never think to look.

ONE YEAR LATER:

"Did anyone order the 20 pans of crab legs that I requested a week ago?" Dream asked while she continued to decorate.

"Yeah, I did," Zeke replied.

Why the hell hasn't Autumn sent something to let me know that she's OK? Zeke thought as he slid through the streets of Atlanta. "Take A Shot For Me" by Drake filled the speakers inside of Dream's X5. Zeke headed to grab Dream's order that she requested and was tempted to drive by his old condo. He couldn't touch anything that belonged to him. It had been a whole year since he drove any of his cars or walked inside his own condo. He cut up all his credit and debit cards. Zeke had not been in the best head space since Autumn disappeared.

Damn, back in the hood, Zeke thought to himself in disbelief. Zeke quickly returned with Dream's order. As he put three pans down, Dream scanned his entire body, looking for any signs of danger. Dream always had Zeke's back. For the last year, she had let him hide in the small apartment that was attached to her house. She knew he wouldn't be safe anywhere else.

"BRANDON!!! Help him bring the rest of those inside of the house!" Dream demanded.

Dream's birthday party was planned for the next day. She was like a bridezilla. "12 hours and counting! 12 hours and counting! Get to work! This has to be just right!" she demanded while sipping on a glass of champagne.

Zeke had other plans for Dream's birthday weekend. He was about to turn this weekend up a couple of notches for her. Both of Dream's homegirls had flown in for the weekend to celebrate her.

Mercedes had arrived first, flying in from Cali. She was five feet, five inches tall, with brown eyes. Mercedes's perfect Coca-Cola bottle shape made her a showstopper. Her plump, round booty complemented her voluptuous curves; her sandy brown hair with blond highlights made her look even more exotic. Mercedes was a video vixen and she was well-known in the industry. She was a long-haired, thick redone, and she was here to set Atlanta on fire.

Dream, Brandon and Zeke had been planning for this b-day bash for about a month now and it was finally here. Zeke also had a couple of tricks up his sleeve.

When she sees the size of these diamond earrings, she might have a heart attack. Zeke thought to himself in excitement.

"The diamond earrings glisten from every angle. Dream deserves these five-carat diamond earrings," Zeke said to himself while he placed them back inside of the box after admiring them.

"We're going to need more balloons," Brandon suggested.

"I can go and get them," Keisha offered.

Keisha was Dream's other homegirl who flew in from New York City. Unlike Mercedes, Keisha came with a different vibe; she was sweet and homely. She didn't wear much makeup and allowed her natural beauty to shine.

Keisha was a plastic surgeon at the age of 29. She had beauty, brains and a career. This was the type of woman you could bring home to Mama. Keisha's skin looked like fresh mocha mixed with honey. She had a certain glow that you don't see often. Keisha was about five feet, four inches tall, and had the frame of a Caucasian woman. She didn't have much booty or many curves, but her bust size made up for what she lacked. Her shape didn't take anything away from her; instead, it gave her character.

Keisha's shoulder-length hair looked silky and black. Her silky bangs moved with each and every head gesture she made. She had the most radiant smile; it reminded everyone she met of shooting stars. Keisha carried herself with class and precision. She made a great first impression, and the first impression means everything.

"Can you drive Keisha to the party store?" Dream asked Zeke.

"I can handle it, Dream. I'm a big girl," Keisha said as she walked out the door.

Zeke quickly followed behind her as she was walking out of Dream's house. He quickly intercepted Dream's key fob out of her hand. Keisha looked up at Zeke and flashed him a quick smile.

The ride to the party store was silent, yet relaxing. Zeke quickly glanced over at Keisha and, to his surprise, she was taking a nap. *She must've been tired*. Zeke's thoughts were quickly interrupted by the sounds of his cellular device. Once he grabbed the device out of his pocket, he took a quick glance at the screen, then immediately focused his eyes back on the road. The incoming call read, "Private Number." Zeke almost hit the "ignore" button, but his spirit told him otherwise.)

"Hello?" Zeke answered in suspense, not knowing who was on the other end.

"I'm flying into town this weekend," Autumn said with excitement in her voice.

Zeke didn't know how to feel in the present moment. He didn't think he would ever hear from her again.

"What day are you flying in?" Zeke asked. Just hearing her voice, he felt a year's worth of dead weight fall from his shoulders.

"I will let you know when I arrive," Autumn said.

Suddenly, the line went blank.

"Hello? Hello?!" Zeke called desperately. He then quickly disconnected after he heard the dial tone.

"Why are you yelling?" Keisha asked in a soft tone of voice.

Zeke didn't reply. He put on the turn signal and turned into the plaza. "We have arrived," he whispered while putting the SUV in park.

''Same Damn Time" by Future filled the speakers inside Dream's house. "Happy birthday, Dream!" yelled the DJ.

Everyone continued to vibe to the track he was playing. Dream's house party was a whole mood and a total vibe.

The bar that Dream had gotten professionally installed for the party had built-in strobe lights and it was filled with different kinds of exclusive liquor. Brandon spent a cool three thousand dollars on all types of fresh fish, crab legs, shrimp and different side dishes such as corn and red baked potatoes. Dream's 25th birthday party was exactly what Zeke needed to loosen up. Over the past couple of months, his life wasn't *his* life.

When Zeke walked through the crowd, his vision was slightly compromised by the Ray-Bans that lay perfectly on his face. He immediately removed the glasses that blocked his vision. The Patrón mixed with the rosé that he had been sippin' on all night had him feeling real wavy. He had to pull himself together, and quickly; he needed to focus on the crowd just in case someone decided to show up.

During the celebration of Dream's birthday, Zeke had forgotten about all his troubles and pain. He couldn't remember the last time he had this much fun. The vibes and energy were so lit. Zeke had even let his guard down for a brief moment. He suddenly spotted a pair of familiar eyes lurking throughout the crowd.

"Was that Yasmeen?" Zeke asked himself while smoothly walking through the crowd to get a closer look.

When he made it to the other side of the room, he carefully scanned each and every visible corner of the house. To Zeke's eyes, nothing looked suspicious and no one looked suspect. He looked over to the right and watched as a couple of girls vibed to the music.

"Am I losing it?" Zeke asked himself while finishing the remainder of his drink.

Zeke attempted to make his way to the bar to grab another drink, but was briefly delayed by a girl who bumped into him. She had accidentally spilled her drink on his all-white Balmain jeans.

"I'm sorry," said the girl. She then quickly disappeared into the crowd.

Zeke quickly reached inside the pockets of his white and burgundy letterman jacket to ensure that everything was still there. He scanned his all-white V-neck and his tan Polo boots, checking to see if his attire had been ruined by the spilled drink.

After doing a body check, Zeke reached into the pockets of his jeans to ensure that the key to Dream's presidential suite was still there. He quickly reached into his other pocket, feeling for the box that held Dream's diamond earrings.

While Zeke continued bobbing his head to the beat, he spotted Keisha slightly stumbling down the stairs. Zeke quickly made his way through the crowd and headed towards her.

Wow, I'm feeling slightly tipsy, Keisha thought to herself while carefully walking down the stairs.

She tried to grab onto the railing, but she was a little too late, because she tripped on an unknown object.

"Ahhhh!" Keisha screamed as she fell into Zeke's arms. "Thank you, Zeke," she said with a sense of relief.

Once Zeke put her down, she wrapped her arms around his neck and gently kissed him on the check.

"You're my hero," Keisha whispered into his right ear softly.

Keisha continued to hold Zeke and the energy between the two was heating up like a pot of stew on a cold winter afternoon. Zeke's thoughts were immediately interrupted as an extremely powerful surge of energy shot through him like an arrow. The energy felt familiar and comforting at the same time. When he turned around to see where this was coming from, he froze in his tracks as he stared into the eyes of the most beautiful woman in the world.

He admired her like a beautiful portrait that hung perfectly on the wall of an art museum. He continued staring into her captivating brown eyes and his empty cold heart began to melt, but what he didn't realize was how enraged Autumn really was. The energy that was illuminating off of her was enough to set Dream's entire house on fire. While Zeke continued to admire Autumn's undeniably and irresistible beauty, she kept her arms folded very tightly and dismissed his lustful eyes. The expression on her face said everything, but Zeke was so blinded by the way she radiated that he missed all the signs. Autumn quickly moved around Zeke and mashed Keisha's head into the nearest wall with excessive force.

"What in the HELL is happening here?!" Autumn screamed.

Zeke was in such a trance that he didn't even notice all the signs of anger she had shown. Before she could throw another punch, Zeke picked her up and carried her into a quiet bathroom upstairs.

Autumn had been through hell and back over the past year. She went off the grid as Zeke instructed; she fled the USA and was secretly transported to a private overseas island. Autumn kept telling herself that this was going to be like going on a beautiful vacation. When she approached the airstrip, her heart pounded. She knew once she got on that plane, there would be no turning back...

"It's going to be OK," Autumn's stepmother had told her with a supportive smile.

Autumn had lost her father and mother many years ago. Her mother died first and her father remarried Samantha, but four years into his second marriage, he died from a broken heart. Autumn and her stepmother, Samantha, never really saw eye to eye, but who *ever* sees eye to eye with their stepparents? Samantha was extremely connected; she was tied in with the CIA and had access to all the top government officials. Autumn didn't want to get her stepmother involved with her personal affairs, but she had no other choice, because this truly was a life-or-death situation. The stubborn young woman always told herself that she would hang herself before she would ever ask Samantha for help. But as you can see, she didn't hang herself, did she? When Autumn entered the unmarked aircraft, she looked back at Samantha. She couldn't see her eyes, but she saw venom pumping through her veins. Samantha let her guard down for a brief moment. Autumn was finally out of her hair, and at her departure revealed Samantha's true intentions. Autumn immediately felt that something wasn't right in the atmosphere. Once her spirit spoke to her, she tried to quickly exit the unmarked aircraft, but was instantly sedated by a dart to the neck that was filled with tranquilizers.

10 HOURS LATER:

"Get up! Get up!" a guard woman yelled with a heavy accent, one that Autumn couldn't make out.
"Where am I?" the drugged, confused and half-awake Autumn asked in panic.

"Get up!" the woman repeated.

The guard grabbed Autumn by the arm very aggressively and forced her to stand.

Autumn rocked side to side as she tried to catch her balance. The guard grabbed her arm and helped Autumn exit the aircraft. When she exited the aircraft, two other guards grabbed her by the arms and forced her into an unmarked SUV.

SLAM!

Autumn jumped at the amount of force that was used to shut the door. She tried to come to her senses, but the tranquilizers were still pumping in her blood. As the SUV sped off, Autumn passed out cold.

This private island is heavily guarded and there's no way to escape, Autumn thought as she rocked back and forth on her bed. She had done lots of research on this place, and what she knew was that everyone on the island was clueless; nobody knew where they were. Most didn't care because they were there due to witness protection. The location was unknown. While being transported, passengers couldn't see out of the windows of the plane nor the SUV because they had tints on them The island enforced strict rules. It was beautiful, but it was a prison. The guards controlled what residents ate and how they dressed; they even had the island on curfew, never allowing residents to walk the island at night. For many months, Autumn always felt like she was being followed. When she first arrived on the island, she went through her own fair share of depression, but she was a survivor by nature.

I hope you're safe, Zeke, Autumn thought to herself as she shed a tear.

Autumn hated Samantha for tricking her like that, but at least she was not in the hands of Mr. Henderson. That's what she told herself to deal with her current situation. The ocean and the beauty that the island offered helped, too.

ONE YEAR LATER:

"HEY!" Autumn screamed.

"What's your problem?" the scared-looking nerd asked in fear.

"I saw that," Autumn whispered.

"Get away from me," the boy genius whined while trying to escape.

Autumn wasn't taking no bullshit; she quickly focused and stopped the nerd in his tracks.

"Hey, what's going on?" the nerd asked in confusion. "Why can't I move?"

Autumn was shocked. She couldn't believe it actually worked.

She had been doing lots of meditation exercises and she also utilized her time cleansing her chakras. Her third eye had been activated; while tapping into her higher self, this gave her the strength to master her psychic abilities.

"Unhand me!" the boy demanded while trying to break free.

"I'm not touching you," Autumn said calmly.

"What do you want?" he asked, this time in a panic.

"I want to know who you are. Who sent you? How did you get a cell phone? Nobody has one of these… You have to be a spy. Now, spill it, or I will make your brain explode," Autumn lied… or did she? "Or," she continued, "I could just tell the guards that you have a cellular device. I'm pretty sure that would be a big violation. What would they do with you?"

"OK! OK! I will tell you everything… Your stepmother, Samantha, sent me here. I'm a hacker. I hacked into a couple of business accounts and transferred a couple million dollars in some private offshore accounts. The accounts were fakes; they were accounts made by Samantha to catch people like me so she could use us as puppets later. When I was being transported to the Feds, Samantha cut me a deal."

"What was the deal?!" Autumn interrupted.

"To spy… on you, and report your whereabouts. That's all I know. Now, unhand me!" the boy demanded!

Suddenly, the air on the island changed and Autumn began to open her eyes. She noticed that most of the people here looked like they were tired all the time and they all seemed to have a very high IQ.

"What's really happening on this island? How many others are there like you?" she asked.

"They would kill me!" the boy cried.

"What's your name?" Autumn asked.

"My name is Franky," he replied.

Autumn didn't know how it happened, but the nerd was suddenly released from her grasp. She hadn't fully mastered her abilities yet. Autumn was still shocked that she was able to do that. She had been reading minds since she was old enough to write, but this was different, and it felt good.

"Show me who Samantha really is and we both will get off this island. You will be a free man."

Franky liked Autumn's deal; he didn't like being Samantha's puppet. Samantha was running a dirty operation. She would find the world's top Hackers, set them up and then force them to steal millions of dollars for her.

"Shhhh," Franky said while showing Autumn lots of footage. Autumn looked at Franky's device, her eyes growing bigger and bigger. Samantha's operation was impressive, but creepy. Autumn watched at least 30 people on the computer stealing money for Samantha for countless hours.

"We never get a break," Franky said while wiping sweat from his face.

"Well, today, you just got a break," Autumn replied while putting a hand on Franky's shoulders.

"Hello?! Why are you calling me? You should be working!" yelled Samantha.

"Samantha, you have been very busy."

"Autumn?!" Samantha said, shocked. She held the phone on the other end in fear and disbelief. She knew that Autumn knew *something,* but how much *did* she know?"When I get a hold of

Franky, he will never see daylight again," she said, trying to take charge of the situation.

The only person that won't be seeing daylight is *you*. I'll tell you what, get me off this island immediately or I'm sending these videos to the CIA. I can't believe you've been using CIA resources to set up your own operations of thieves."

"Hush! And don't you say another word. I will have you off the island in the next couple of hours," Samantha said with lots of sense.

"Franky is coming, too," Autumn demanded.

"Autumn, you're pushing it. You don't understand what you're getting involved in. This is bigger than you think," Samantha said on the other end while dismissing herself from FBI Agent Jones's office.

"Let's see how big this is when the CIA finds out what you've been doing," Autumn threatened.

"OK. I will have you *and* him transported to the airstrip." Samantha discontinued the call. She knew what she had to do. "There's a rat in the bunch," she said while entering the unmarked car of CIA Agent Dixon. "Take me to the private airstrip," she commanded Agent Dixon.

TWO HOURS LATER:

Autumn and Franky felt a sense of relief as they prepared to exit the island. Franky hugged Autumn tightly and thanked her.

"No problem," Autumn replied.

"Sit down!" Samantha demanded.

The three of them looked at each other in suspense. Autumn

had realized how long she'd been disconnected from the world; when she looked at Samantha's freshly manicured nails, it complemented her fresh facial which had her skin glowing. The fresh scent of hair care products bought her a sense of peace. She wore a pair of red bottom heels that screamed "fuck me" and tied in very well with her expensive tailored black suit. Autumn immediately looked at her gear, and the rags she wore suddenly irritated her skin. As she stroked her hair, it felt rough, dry and mistreated. *I can't wait to go to the hair salon,* Autumn said to herself very self-consciously. At that moment, Autumn felt many mixed emotions. She wanted to choke the shit out of Samantha, but kept her cool.

Boom! Boom!

Autumn's thoughts were suddenly interrupted as she watched Samantha put two slugs into Franky's head,.Blood splashed in Autumn's face as she watched in terror.

"I hate rats," Samantha muttered as she put her gun away.

"Oh! Autumn, did you *really* think I would let him live so he could take me down later? You should know best to always take out your enemy," Samantha laughed. "I'm not going to kill you. We will make a deal, though," she said.

"Why would I ever want to make a deal with you?" Autumn said while removing Franky's blood from her face.

"You already made a deal with me when you stepped on my jet."

Autumn's eyes grew extremely big. She knew the lady was loaded, but not *this* loaded.

"Autumn, you are still my daughter," Samantha said in a loving tone.

"Stepdaughter! And *never* forget that," Autumn barked.

"I will help you take out your enemy and set you up with enough cash to start a new life."

"Why would you help me?" Autumn asked in disbelief.

"That's what family is for," she replied while opening a bottle of expensive champagne.

"Family would never throw family on an island and abandon them!" Autumn yelled. "You tried to get rid of me!"

"Well, I didn't try to get rid of you completely. I took you to a safe place, did I not? I see that you're still alive," Samantha said. She finished her glass of champagne, then continued in a sinister voice. "Enough of the small talk. You need me to clean up your mess, and I need you to shut your mouth and never repeat what you saw! Do we have a deal?"

Autumn knew she had no choice but to continue dancing with the devil for now.

Samantha gave Autumn a debit card and a burner cell phone.

"What do I do with this?" Autumn asked.

"That's how we will communicate! Your friend Mr. Henderson is very dangerous. Even if I locked him up right now, that wouldn't stop him from murdering you. He can touch anyone," Samantha said while fixing herself another drink.

Zeke thought he was the only person who had it rough over the last past year. He didn't know that Autumn had endured much worse. When he looked more deeply into her eyes, they told a story: She wasn't the same girl she used to be. Autumn had blossomed into a woman. She was now a trauma survivor; she had just seen Franky murdered right before her eyes one day ago, which had given her a hint of PTSD. When Zeke took a closer look, he could see pain and torment on her face.

Why didn't I see any of this earlier? Zeke thought to himself as he looked at her with pleading eyes.

"I thought you were going to call me when you arrived," Zeke said in an apologetic tone.

"I would've, but I discarded the device I had and I wanted to surprise you," Autumn said suspiciously.

Zeke squinted his eyes while he looked at her. He knew she was hiding something.

"I will tell you all about it later. Let's talk about what I saw downstairs," Autumn said as she rolled her eyes.

"Listen, Autumn. Lots of things have taken place in my life. My sister's husband got busted by the Feds the other day."

"What does that have to do with anything?!" Autumn quickly interrupted.

"Can you let me finish, please?" Zeke asked.

"I'm listening!" Autumn said with lots of aggravation in her voice.

"The Feds are now after me. My mom called me yesterday and informed me that nine black unmarked cars surrounded her house."

Zeke was being very dismissive of the current situation at hand. He had been moving recklessly. His plate was too full, which clouded his thoughts and judgment. To him, everybody was suspect or out to destroy him. He hadn't slept in weeks, which was causing him to hallucinate. He wanted nothing more than for all these events to just disappear; they were taking a big toll on his complicated and disturbed life.

"What the hell were you doing, holding that trick?" Autumn asked, this time raising her voice.

"Listen! Autumn, that was nothing. I'm kinda faded and I don't feel like arguing. All I want to do is get more wasted and have drunk sex," Zeke replied as he pulled Autumn onto his lap.

"Do you wanna have drunk sex with *her*?" Autumn asked in a seductive tone.

"Shut up and kiss me! I've missed you," Zeke said while holding Autumn tightly.

Autumn hadn't been touched by anyone sexually in a long time. His touches instantly made her flinch. She had forgotten how good Zeke's hands felt on her soft skin. Zeke wrapped his arms around her waist, and her soft, warm skin felt pleasant in his hands.

Once their lips touched, chills ran through their bodies. As their tongues touched, Zeke gently placed her on the edge of the sink. Anticipation quickly flooded the small bathroom as their bodies and souls yearned for one another. When his soft lips met her neck, she let out sweet, soft moans. Zeke continued to trail kisses up her neck and she immediately dug her nails into his back. Her nails digging into his skin silently turned him on; he grabbed her face to look into her soul and she kissed him even more passionately, then closed her eyes while their lips made love. She *needed* him inside of her and he *wanted* to be inside of her! She wrapped her legs around him and began rolling her hips slowly. This motion was about to make him explode. He felt the heat illuminating off of her precious flower.

Autumn's plump lips felt like heaven to him and his to her. The amount of passion that they were sharing inside the small bathroom was slightly uncomfortable for them both, but they didn't care. They'd missed each other and they needed each other at this moment.

"Mmm!" Autumn moaned while grabbing his throbbing

shaft.

Zeke quickly loosened her buttons and unzipped her zipper. When he put his hands on her once more, she let out moans that were soft, but massive. He then gently used both of his fingers to part her lips; her insides felt wet, warm and untouched. He quickly tried to remove her jeans and she held his hard, throbbing shaft into her hands. She wasn't going to let it go until he was inside of her...

BOOM! BOOM! BOOM!

"Open my damn door NOW!!! I *know* you are in there!" Dream yelled as she continued to bang on the door like a madwoman.

Autumn quickly fastened her jeans and jumped down off the sink.

"Wait! What are you doing?" Zeke asked in desperation.

"Move!" Autumn said while opening the door. "Happy birthday, Dream!" she shouted, smiling at Dream.

"Don't wish me a happy birthday. Who the hell do you think you are?" Dream asked, invading Autumn's personal space. "What made you think it was OK to attack my friend inside *my* house at *my* party? I should rock you just for being disrespectful."

"Dream, it's your day, and you're totally right. I overreacted. I apologize," Autumn said while holding back her wrath.

Dreamed rolled her eyes at Autumn and turned to Zeke. "Really? This is all your fault, Zeke."

Zeke said nothing; the only thing on this mind was Autumn. Everything Dream said during her lecture went in one ear and out the other.

"Handle your shit better!" Dream yelled, trying to make herself heard over the loud music that was playing. When she walked past Zeke, she brushed him with excessive force.

TWO HOURS LATER:

"My President Is Black" by JAY-Z filled the speakers inside the bar that Dream's husband had rented for her after-party. Everybody who was at Dream's house party was now at the bar. This party was not stopping until the sun came up. The vibrations in the after-party were lit; all eyes were on Dream and Mercedes. As Dream adjusted her crown that read "Birthday Bitch," three sexy waitresses, dressed in all-black lingerie, came dancing through the crowd with Dream's favorite liquor and a huge banner that read "Happy Birthday." The bottles that they carried came with a very entertaining light show. The DJ quickly remixed the "Happy Birthday" song while the bottles were being delivered to Dream's VIP section. The three sexy waitresses did a sexy dance routine until the flares burned out. They placed the bottles on the table and made a sexy exit through the crowd. Dream wasn't expecting that to happen.

"Hell fuckin' yeah!" Dreamed yelled in excitement while Mercedes poured liquor right from the bottle down Dream's throat. Autumn didn't feel comfortable at the party as she eyed Keisha. Keisha grilled her back.

"Is there a problem here?" Dreamed asked as she felt the vibes in the section.

After everything Autumn had been through, she couldn't take the attitude or the hate she was feeling. The series of events that had taken place over the past year was beginning to affect her mood.

I'm about to bust Dream and Keisha in the head with one of these damn bottles, Autumn thought to herself before she stormed out of the bar.

Zeke watched as Autumn disappeared through the crowd. He

wanted to run behind her, but at that moment, all he wanted to do was vibe with Dream; it was her birthday celebration, after all. *How could she show up after a year and bring unnecessary drama? Why couldn't she just vibe with me and ignore the BS? I'm not chasing her and she's not gonna kill my vibes*, Zeke thought as he dismissed the situation.

(Stop!!! Look!!! Wait a minute and let me bring you up to speed. Zeke also had a lot of things on his plate. It's true that Autumn needed him, but at the time, he couldn't respond to her properly.

Zeke needed to readjust; then, he could be well-equipped to fulfill Autumn's requirements as a man supposed to be. Readers, understand that Zeke is not an unjust or uncivilized man.

Once again, he just wanted to enjoy his weekend, but Autumn was adding additional problems. All he wanted was to simply relax, unwind and have some time for himself, then deal with all problems and issues on Monday. Zeke's only one man, and that one man is no good to anyone without proper care and love for himself first.)

"I have a surprise for you," Zeke said to Dream while handing her a small white envelope.

Before she opened the white envelope, she glanced at Zeke in suspense. He began to laugh uncontrollably at the sight of Dream's face; she acted as if the envelope contained a million-dollar check in it. Dream, too, began to laugh. She couldn't remember the last time she heard Zeke laugh. Dream knew that he had been so consumed with many different issues, so to see him loosening up brought her joy.

She opened the small envelope and pulled out a hotel key. Her smile instantly grew wider. She then investigated the envelope and spotted Zeke's handwriting on the inside in the top right hand corner. It read:

Happy birthday, Dream. The key you have in your hand goes to an exclusive presidential suite that overlooks downtown.

She quickly hugged Zeke while thanking him multiple times. When she removed her arms from around him, she screamed so loudly that everyone who was in earshot turned around to see what all the commotion was about. Dream jumped up and down in the VIP section like she had just hit the jackpot. Zeke had given her the diamond earrings that he was carrying all night.

"Damn, girl. Those look pretty expensive," Mercedes said as she examined the diamonds Dream pulled out of the box.

"How many carats are they?" Mercedes asked Zeke while Dream removed her old earrings and put the new ones on.

"Five!" said Zeke humbly.

"Thank you! Thank you," Dreamed said as she kissed Zeke on the cheek.

While Zeke sat at the bar, he looked at his phone in hopes he would have received a text or call from Autumn, but to his surprise, there were neither.

"Can I buy you a drink?" Keisha asked, joining Zeke at the

bar.

"Can *you* buy *me* a drink?" Zeke replied, laughing.

"What are you laughing at?" Keisha asked, not understanding the joke.

"It's just funny, 'cause I have a rule," he replied, this time in a serious tone.

"What kind of rule?" she asked while turning into her chair to face him.

"A lady never pays for her own drink," he replied smoothly.

"That's sweet. However, I don't mind. Mama has her own funds and I'm not one of these ratchet girls in here. So, if you don't mind, sit back and let someone take care of you. I've watched you take care of everyone else. Now, it's your turn to let someone take care of you," she replied very seductively. "Now, what would you like to drink?"

I'm going against all rules here, Zeke thought to himself in disbelief. She wanted to buy him a drink, and besides, her bravery was kinda exciting. Plus, she wasn't taking no for an answer.

"Patrón. We're going to drink Patrón," Zeke replied, hesitating.

"I'm not much of a drinker, but I'll have a drink with you," Keisha said as she ordered for the both of them.

All night, while Zeke looked into Keisha's eyes, his mind began to drift and it was like he was looking into the eyes of Autumn. Their minds, bodies and souls were so intertwined; it was as if they were one. Somehow, throughout the night, Autumn's presence was revolving around him. Maybe Zeke had too much to drink. He tried to silence his emotions, yet he couldn't. What Zeke didn't know was that Autumn had gotten stronger than he had imagined. It felt as if she was intercepting his activities—that is, any activities she didn't want him to take part in.

THE NEXT MORNING:

Zeke was awoken by an unfamiliar presence that rested peacefully next to him. He wiped his hungover eyes to make sure he wasn't hallucinating. As his vision became clear, he knew that it wasn't Autumn who lay next to him. He quickly lifted the blankets that covered them and, to his surprise, both of them were fully dressed in the same outfits they had on last night. Zeke's sudden movements awoke Keisha. She reached over and wrapped her arms around him.

He quickly sat up and asked, "Did we?"

"Nothing happened. You were extremely drunk and what I remember is us falling asleep," she said softly.

Faithful men and women, if you have ever cheated before, I'm not judging you. But if you feel the need to cheat, you might want to reassess your values in your current relationship, 'cause there's obviously something you should try to work out with the one you love. Personally, I would never take someone's hand in marriage if I could see myself sleeping with someone else. To me, that means they're not the one for me.

"I'm not blaming anything on the liquor because that would be too typical. This can't happen. It wasn't even supposed to go this far," Zeke said while trying not to hurt her feelings.

She looked at him with pleading eyes; she felt small and worthless in the moment. The very first day she laid eyes on him, she thought he was the perfect man. Keisha had been waiting on her opportunity to make her move, not even knowing he was in love with someone else.

"You really love her?" Keisha asked while putting distance between them.

We have all been in situations where our loyalty was tested. Always remember that it's not about the mistake you made or the mistake you were about to make. It really boils down to what's really in your heart—*that's* what truly matters. Whether you're thinking about your spouse in the moment, you're a person who lives in the moment and deals with the drama later if you're caught, or maybe you're just on #TeamFuckIt, the creator judges the heart. That's all that matters; no one can judge anyone else.

Remember that all are needed by all because nothing is fair or good alone, for we are one like the grains of sand in the hourglass. Love is to be special; love is to be bold and potent. But what *is* love? Now, I always say it is synonymous to trust. There is a circular relationship between trust and integrity, as trust is essentially a reliance on another's integrity. Healthy children will not fear life if their elders have integrity enough not to fear death.

LEGEND

"Zeke, I've never met a man like you," Keisha said as she left the bedroom.

20 MINUTES LATER:

When they arrived at the airport, Keisha was having mixed emotions because she still wanted more time with Zeke, but she knew that wasn't possible. Sadness showed on her face while Zeke grabbed her suitcase out of the back seat.

"Thanks for driving me to the airport," Keisha said as she grabbed her rolling suitcase.

"No problem," Zeke said while entering the SUV.

"If y'all don't work out, you have my number," Keisha said. She then blew Zeke a kiss and made her way inside the airport.

Zeke put his head on the headrest for a brief moment and was interrupted by the voice of a police officer.

"Sir, you can't sit here. Please keep moving," the officer said aggressively.

Now Watch it Unfold

CHAPTER 3
THE LIGHT IN THE DARKNESS MEETS THE GATEKEEPER

DAY TWO OF DREAM'S BIRTHDAY WEEKEND:

"Sexual Healing" by Marvin Gaye filled the speakers inside Dream's house. She was in the middle of the floor, sitting in a chair like a queen on her throne. Dream's all-black BEBE cocktail dress that cost $2,000 laid on her body like a second layer of skin. Her long, black, curly hair complemented her makeup that had been professionally done hours ago. She looked absolutely stunning—a true Black Barbie would be the proper title.

The diamond earrings that Zeke bought her blinged with each and every movement she made. On her neck lay a beautiful 22-karat gold, diamond-studded necklace that Brandon had surprised her with, not to mention she had on some black and gold exclusive BEBE pumps that gave her outfit the right touch. While she adjusted the diamond-studded crown that lay perfectly on the top of her head, she continued sipping out of her champagne glass. The DJ switched the track to Rihanna's "Cockiness"—"I love it, I love it, I love it when you eat it." It was a special request; Brandon knew what his wife liked. Mercedes walked seductively as she approached Dream. Dream looked at her and instantly felt the vibe. Mercedes began giving her the best lap dance that she had ever experienced. When Mercedes dropped down, she opened Dream's legs and put her head between them. Mercedes then sat on Dream's lap and started grinding seductively to the beat. Once the chorus played, she bounced up and down while making it clap.

"Somebody bring me some $10s and $20s!" Dreamed yelled as Mercedes continued rolling her hips better than any stripper. Dream gripped Mercedes's round apple, then pulled her in for a kiss. When the music stopped, everyone applauded them for their performance.

TWO HOURS LATER:

"Tonight is about to be epic," Dream said as she packed an overnight bag.

"I'm going to show you how we party in California," Mercedes said while taking more shots.

"You are not ready!" Brandon teased Mercedes as he juggled a bag full of ecstasy pills.

"Do those things actually work?" Zeke asked with a curious mind.

"That's a stupid question to ask! Every drink at Dream's party was laced with those things, " said Autumn as she walked through the front door.

Zeke was extremely confused. He hadn't heard from her since the other night when she stormed out of the bar.

"Dream invited me here," Autumn said while rolling her neck seductively and batting her eyelashes slowly.

Autumn came prepared to impress. Her scent was very captivating; she smelled like a field of fresh flowers on a cool summer day. Autumn's silky, straight hair followed down past her waistline. She wore a pair of cream high-waisted jeans that hugged her physique, showing every curve she had to offer. The red bottom pumps that she had on were covered in diamond-studded spikes that sparkled naturally. Her perky breasts spoke to you through the all-white crop top that laid on her skin like fine silk. She was glowing like a full moon on a cool summer night at the beach.

Looks like she's been pampering herself, Zeke thought to himself as the model approached him.

"I apologize about the other night," Autumn said while hugging her man tightly.

Watching Franky get murdered right before her very own eyes had greatly affected her. She just needed a little bit of time to put those thoughts to rest because they were getting the best of her.

"I'm ready for you," Autumn said, kissing Zeke on the lips very passionately.

Autumn had a surprise guest with her whom nobody had ever seen before. Her name was Kelly; she was a Caucasian woman that stood at five feet, five inches with a pair of ocean blue eyes that matched her perfectly bleached blonde hair. Her hair was pulled into a ponytail, which gave her a soft and innocent demeanor, like that of a librarian.

Who is Kelly? And is she as innocent as she looks? Zeke asked himself while secretly cross-examining Kelly.

"Have you worked in the library before?" Mercedes asked Kelly.

"The—the library?" Kelly stuttered.

"Just loosen up and let your hair down, baby," said Mercedes with a smile that could end world hunger.

"Who is that?" Brandon asked Zeke while pulling him into a more private setting.

"I wasn't done talking!" Autumn said as Brandon and Zeke exited the house.

"Me, Dream, you, Autumn, Kelly and Mercedes in one room. This sounds like trouble," Brandon said with a devilish grin.

"What sounds like trouble? And why y'all outside? Y'all look like y'all plotting on something," Dream said as she headed to the SUV with her overnight bag.

"Practice" by Drake played on the radio as they all headed towards downtown. "Let's play a game," Mercedes said while turning down the radio.

"What's the game?" Kelly asked as she took a couple puffs of the perfectly-rolled blunt that was being passed around.

"We're going to play truth or dare," Mercedes said, taking the blunt out of Kelly's hand.

"What's the dare?" Brandon asked as he turned into the hotel parking lot.

"I dare everyone in this vehicle to take one full ecstasy pill. If you don't do the dare, then you have to do something super embarrassing when we enter the Hotel lobby."

Brandon passed everyone a pill, and one by one, each person in the friend group took theirs. "See how fun that was?,"Mercedes grinned as they exited the SUV.

"Front desk. How may I help you?" asked the polite receptionist.

"Can I place an order?" Zeke asked.

"I can take your order when you're ready, sir," she replied very helpfully.

"Can I have 10 shots of Ciroc, 10 shots of Patrón and a big bowl of mixed fruit," Zeke said while watching everybody's vibe.

30 MINUTES LATER:

"Oh! We have a mini bar full of liquor!" Mercedes exclaimed while throwing everybody a personal shot bottle.

After a couple of shots and five blunts later, Mercedes stripped down in an all-black Victoria's Secret lace panty and bra set. She cleared the desk and then turned on R. Kelly›s "Slow Wind." She jumped on the desk and gave the entire room a show. Dream pulled the curtains back, relieving the downtown view. The city view glistened off of her perfect silhouette. The light that came from the moon shone and sparkled on her sweet, soft, and vanilla silk skin...

She looked at everyone in the room seductively as she rubbed her body up and down; her hands making their way down to her thong. She then pulled it down just a little bit, giving everyone a simple tease. Dropping to her knees, she started spinning her head around while popping her ass in a slow rotation to the beat. Getting on all fours, she allowed her face to meet the desk while putting a deep arch in her back and rolling her hips some more to the beat. She sure showed the crowd that she knew how to throw it back. When the show ended, everyone applauded.

Mercedes then grabbed an all-white robe and put it over her body. Dream then walked to the bedroom to seduce the situation. She called Kelly to the bedroom; she'd been striking Dream›s attention ever since she walked through the front door. Kelly laid on the bed and Dream began giving her a back massage. Dream instructed Kelly to take off her bra. At this point, Brandon and Mercedes joined them in the bed, as well. Zeke and Autumn were on the pull-out bed in the living room of the presidential suite. The living room and the master suite were right next to each other; the only thing that separated the two was a huge, fancy wet bar. As they kissed very passionately, Zeke laid on top of Autumn's soft and warm skin. His hands cuffed her cheeks as he lifted her up a little just to get a better clearance. He slowly entered her sweet, wet, tight, tender walls. Autumn felt her insides stretching as she began to gasp for air. Zeke went even deeper inside; with every thrust, he got harder and harder. Autumn began pulling Zekes dreadlocks very seductively while licking her lips.

We are going to keep the rest private. My apologies to the readers—just keep reading. This story gets better and better.

Zeke and Autumn lay in a hot tub full of love and bubbles and held each other very passionately as the water sparkled off their skin. Zeke began to kiss Autumn's neck while the steam coming from the hot tub soothed their minds, bodies and souls.

"I saw a man… die… right before my very own eyes!" Autumn said while wiggling her toes in the hot tub. "Samatha had me kidnapped and locked up on a private island full of her hacker slaves."

"What!?" Zeke asked in confusion. "Why didn't you tell me sooner?!" Someone began to bang on the bathroom door..

"Who is it?" Zeke asked.

"Come walk downstairs with me!!!" Brandon yelled as he burst through the bathroom door.

"Give me a minute! And why did you burst through the door like that? We could've been doing anything!" Zeke replied while covering Autumn.

"Hahaha! Y'all ain't no fun," Brandon joked, then closed the door behind him.

Autumn grabbed Zeke's hands while tears rolled down her face. Brandon's brief interruption had only numbed the pain for a quick second.

"Autumn, babe! We will make her pay," Zeke said as he wiped away her tears.

"No, no, no… We have to let her live for now! Go check on Brandon. I'm going to relax some more inside this hot tub. Just let me gather my thoughts," Autumn said.

Zeke exited the hot tub at Autumn's request, kissed her very passionately, put on his robe, and left the bathroom.

"Brandon, let me find out you're cockblocking," Zeke said, rolling his eyes as they started their journey downstairs. "What's up with Mercedes? And I heard Kelly and Dream," he continued jokingly.

"Now, you *know* Autumn will shut this party down. The FBI's on your trail and we have all types of narcotics in the room. If you fuck this night up for me and Dream, we both gon' kick your ass," Brandon said, laughing at the situation.

"Why are we going to the front desk?" Zeke asked.

"Because I need some condoms," he replied.

"Right, 'cause you don't need any surprises!" Zeke snorted.

"What's up with all these sophisticated words?" Brandon asked.

On their way back upstairs to the room, Zeke spotted Autumn in the hallway. She was sitting with her knees upward towards her chest, crying while having a conversation on a burner phone. Zeke immediately told Brandon he would catch up with him later. He needed to check on Autumn because something strange was happening and he suspected that it had something to do with Samantha. While Autumn spoke to the mysterious person on the phone, a presence entered their circle once more, except this time, it was coming with even more precision and force. Zeke quickly stood up, and at that moment, it was as if someone stopped the hands of time momentarily. He looked to his left and then to his right—everything was completely frozen. Zeke put his hands close to one of the doors in the hallway and felt a sudden surge of heat within the walls of the frozen, gloomy hallways. He then began to choke at the taste of darkness, evil and burning debris!

What is happening here?! Zeke asked himself.

The dark forces that he felt became very clear; it was as if whatever forces had taken hold of him were now controlling the entire environment. He looked back, to his left and then to his right, and thousands of demonic spirits tried to grab a hold of his very essence and soul. The faces of these spirits were something that no one would ever want to see. While continuing down the hall in a complete trance, he turned to the left to see a beast. It was at least seven feet tall with goat feet and huge wings that resembled a very large bat, and it began to charge at him.

"Let's go!" Zeke yelled in panic. As he grabbed Autumn's hand and headed towards the elevator, his heart began to beat faster than any racehorse. Sweat dripped uncontrollably from his face while Autumn looked at him.

"What's going on in this hotel of horror?" she asked.

He quickly pressed the button on the switch marked ''L" for lobby. Once the doors opened, Zeke looked down and the sight that he saw brought chills to his body and soul. He had just seen what they call Hell at his feet. He watched millions of souls crying bloody tears and they screamed to the top of their lungs for help, but nobody answered.

Somebody help these souls, Zeke thought as he watched helplessly.

The inferno that blazed beneath his feet gave him third-degree burns as he walked closer. Here, I'm supposed to express to my readers that we all have different beliefs about what Hell is, but what he saw wasn't a joke—this actual scene took place right before his very eyes. Zeke quickly walked backwards inside the elevator as the sight before him disappeared. The burns on his feet also disappeared and the pain subsided slowly as he put distance between him and the unwanted open portal.

Autumn didn't exit the elevator; instead, she watched in suspense because she couldn't see what he was seeing, but she was feeling every sensation of this intense moment.

"I don't know what you just saw or experienced, but whatever it was, it wasn't right," Autumn said with fear and concern in her voice.

When the elevator arrived on their floor, the doors opened. Zeke peeked his head around the corner, making sure that the coast was clear.

Hmm. Nothing out of the ordinary, Zeke thought as he exited the elevator cautiously.

Did that really happen? Or could it have been the drugs and alcohol that triggered my psychic abilities, creating that vivid scene a few minutes ago? he asked himself in confusion.

Autumn grabbed Zeke's hand to try and make sense of the situation and pulled him back into the hotel room to try to explain to him what was happening with her in the hallway, but couldn't because the mood changed when they entered the presidential suite. They both remembered why they were there.

Autumn was talking to Samantha about something, but why was she crying? Zeke asked himself as her warm hands led him inside the party.

It appeared that nothing had changed in the world of Dream. Everybody was enjoying the party while walking around in thick, all-white plush robes.

Ohhhh! I can get creative with this bowl of fruit, Mercedes thought as she pulled a bag of MDMA out of her lace bra. *This is surely going to spice things up a bit,* she thought while taking the fruit into the master bedroom. She had her own secret agenda.

"Hey, are you OK? You look as if you saw a ghost," Dream asked Zeke as he took down a double shot of tequila.

"Are you enjoying your birthday weekend?" he asked, dismissing her question.

"I'm having a blast," Dream whispered into his ear while hugging him with a thankful spirit.

Autumn began to devour the fruit that was placed inside the master bedroom. The other girls followed suit and began attacking it like wild animals. Mercedes fed Dream several pieces of fruit; each and every one was satisfying to Dream's taste buds. Mercedes continued to laugh on the inside as she enjoyed the scenery, because she knew that she had just done some *serious* damage.

"Zeke, help me! Autumn yelped while reaching for Zeke's hand to help her out of the bed.

The fruit she had just eaten had her on a different level. She was feeling better than ever for some reason. She hadn't felt this good in a long time and all her past demons had suddenly disappeared.

"Are you OK?" Zeke asked as he helped her out of the bed that everybody was laying in.

"Never better, baby. Never better," she replied with a Kool-Aid smile.

"The Morning" by The Weekend filled the speakers inside the hotel room. While Autumn and Zeke passed a Cuban cigar to each other, you could hear Kelly and Mercedes moaning down the hallway.

"Dang, they are not wasting *no* time," Autumn said while she held Zeke tighter.

"Did you see what I saw in the hallway earlier?" Zeke asked.

"No! But whatever it was, I felt it, and it wasn't right," she replied.

He explained every detail from start to finish, and the things he told Autumn were not appealing to her ears. She stopped him mid-sentence because the story was disturbing her mood.

"Please stop," Autumn said, trembling.

"I'm not going to let anything happen to you. I should've never forced you to disappear," Zeke said, feeling guilty.

"Let's just enjoy each other tonight," Autumn said as she hopped on top of him.

THE NEXT MORNING:

"Where are you rushing off to?" Zeke asked Autumn as she got dressed.

"I'm going to have brunch with your sister, Teresa," she replied with a smile.

"When did y'all plan this?" he asked while putting on his Balenciagas.

"She texted me this morning. You know your sister and I haven't really seen eye to eye over the years. It's going to be quite refreshing seeing her. Stay here and help Dream get this place together," she demanded while kissing him on the forehead.

"Hey! Please be careful," Zeke said as he watched those seductive hips exit the hotel.

Zeke, Dream, Brandon, Kelly and Mecedes headed back to Dream's. On the ride, Dream and Mercedes cuddled in the back seat.

"Y'all in love now," Brandon teased while turning into the driveway.

"Last night was epic," Brandon said while opening the front door to his and Dream's house. Loud laughter filled the living room as everybody shared their own personal experiences.

"Yeah, somebody drugged us badly," Dream said as she was suddenly interrupted by Zeke. He put his index finger over his mouth, grabbed his nine-millimeter handgun and peeked through the blinds slowly.

"Who's outside in an all-black Bentley GT with two black hummers following behind it?," he said, trying to identify the tag numbers.

Dream was on her way to get a better look at the vehicles, but was distracted by the sweet smell of fresh lavender on a summer morning. When Mercedes walked down the stairs, she wore a white evening gown. Her hair was pulled back into a sophisticated bun. Her red bottoms sparkled as she lifted her dress lightly so that her clearance would be easy as she made her way down. Mercedes's beauty, grace, elegance and smile stunned the entire room. The diamonds that hung from her ears look like mini chandeliers that glistened naturally.

"Where are you going?" Dream asked while all eyes were on Mercedes.

"I have a date with the Ambassador," Mercedes said, exiting the front door with such elegance and grace.

CHAPTER 4
THE BEHEMOTH VS
THE 7 HEADED BEAST

Meanwhile, somewhere downtown, Teresa and Autumn continued to enjoy their brunch while taking in the summer breeze.

"I'm glad you could join me," said Teresa with a warm and welcoming smile.

"I've been wanting to have a sit-down conversation with you. It's good to see you. What's the glow all about?" Autumn asked with lots of passion, putting her right hand on her chest.

"The glow comes from finding inner peace within myself. Also, I've been living a healthy lifestyle."

They tapped their champagne glasses together, sharing the moment. "How have you and my brother been getting along?" Teresa asked

"We are making it work through all the chaos," Autumn said while eating her vegetarian omelette. The turmeric mixed with spicy vegetables had Autumn's taste buds making love to each other.

"This food is so good! I'm glad we came here," Teresa said. Autumn agreed.

They were suddenly interrupted by two tall, handsome men. One was Spanish and the other was from England; they had on all-black, tailor-made Armani suits. They both had hair that was cut low and wore all-black glasses.

Teresa and Autumn were very surprised as their brunch was interrupted.

"Can we help you two gentlemen?" Teresa asked while slowly reaching inside of her purse. One of the mysterious gentlemen immediately put a gun to Teresa's stomach. Teresa instantly jumped as Autumn began to panic.

"Oh, my God! Are these Mr. Henderson's people?" Autumn asked herself while thinking of a getaway plan.

''Don't move, or I'll blow a hole in your stomach," said one of the gentlemen.

Teresa could have easily sent both of these men to meet their Creator. *Damn, I have a daughter at home*, she thought to herself as she tried to find a more sensible way.

"And if you move, Autumn, I'm pulling the trigger with no hesitation," the other gentleman said.

How does he know my name? Autumn asked herself while trying to find an escape route.

"You two ladies will do exactly what we say and nobody will get hurt. If one of you does anything that we find distasteful, we will not hesitate to end you right here," the tall and handsome Spanish gentleman said while holding his silencer to Autumn's rib cage.

"Walk with us and don't make any sudden movements. We will not repeat ourselves," Said the other gentleman, who looked like he should be on the cover of an exclusive magazine.

The gentlemen forced Teresa and Autumn to intertwine their arms with theirs as if they were on a date. As the two men and two ladies walked very romantically to the parking lot, the two gentlemen kept their silencers pointed toward the ladies' rib cages.

"Can we handle this in a more civilized way? And what is this all about?" Teresa asked.

"Keep moving and keep quiet,". the Spanish gentleman instructed Teresa while forcing his gun deeper into her ribs.

"Ouch! Why are you being so rough? Teresa asked with lots of aggression in her voice.

When they approached the SUV, Teresa turned around and punched the gentleman in the mouth. He then hit Teresa in the face with the butt of his gun. She immediately passed out cold.

"We have to help them!" said CIA Agent Dixon while pulling the hammer back on his pistol.

"No!" Samantha said while finishing her salad.

"Are we just going to let them kidnap those innocent women?" asked Agent Dixon.

Samantha watched the men closely to try and get a good description of them, but was quickly interrupted.

"That's your daughter out there! I will take matters into my own hands. I won't let this happen," said Agent Dixon. He attempted to leave the unmarked vehicle.

"Agent! Don't open that door!" Samantha said, pointing two golden guns at him.

"Put those guns down, Samantha! You know that just as quickly as you can pull that trigger, I can disable those weapons faster," said Agent Dixon while keeping his composure.

"This may be our only opportunity to find Mr. Henderson. Once our guys load them into the SUV, we will trail them," Samantha said, putting her guns back into her holster.

Agent Dixon knew this was very risky. He has never been in the business of gambling with others' lives, but Samantha had a valid point. He wanted to take Mr. Henderson down just as badly as Samantha did.

"AAAHHH!" Autumn screamed as she tried to make a quick getaway.

The Spanish man caught her by the ponytail and quickly put his hand over her mouth. Autumn bit his hand and attempted to run, but her body went completely limp as the gentleman shoved a syringe into her neck.

"This filthy-mouthed human bit me!" he gasped. "You think that I may need a rabies shot?" the man asked his colleague.

"Who cares about your rabies when *this* one has the softest booty I've ever felt?" the man from England said while he eyed Teresa.

The two men loaded the girls inside the all-black SUV, slammed the doors and exited the parking garage, driving into the sunny afternoon.

MEANWHILE, BACK AT DREAM'S HOUSE:

"Zeke, are you OK?" Dream asked.

"I'm OK. I just have a really bad headache," Zeke said as he wiped blood from his nose.

"Zeke! Your nose is bleeding!" Dream said as she scanned the area for a washcloth.

Zeke touched his nostrils and looked at his hands. Blood was everywhere.

Damn, there's nothing in this living room to put on his nose, Dream thought to herself as she immediately ran upstairs to get a washrag.

Sharp pains began to shoot through Zeke's brain; they were powerful enough to make him drop to his knees. The ringing sounds that played in his head were the sounds of a moving freight train that was blowing its horn like it was a serious emergency.

Zeke looked up at Dream as she tried to communicate with him. The only thing he heard was a loud ringing sound; everything around him had gone completely mute. He put his hands over his ears and tried to scream, but nothing came out. *This headache is like none other,* Zeke thought to himself as the headaches became more intense. He started to feel like someone was hitting him in the head with a sledgehammer.

His eyes began to roll into the back of his head as blood began to leak from his ears; he felt as if he had a serious hangover while riding on a merry-go-round. Different objects in the house began to float as the lights in the house flashed on and off.

"What the hell is happening?" Dream asked Brandon as they began to panic and fear for Zeke's life.

Zeke began to see quick flashes of Teresa screaming while being tortured and tormented. Whoever the individuals were, they seemed to enjoy inflicting this pain. Sharp pains continued shooting through his spine like thunder hitting a tree. Both of his hands went numb, and his feet went next. "HEEEYYYY!!!" Dreamed screamed as Zeke passed out cold. "WAKE UP!" she yelled. But he was unresponsive.

Dream paced back and forth, then grabbed her cell phone to dial 911. "What are you doing?" Brandon asked while quickly eliminating the call. "Baby, you can't call 911. He's wanted," he said.

"I know who to call," Dream said while she ran upstairs to grab her burner phone.

"Hello?" Kay answered.

"There are some strange things going on up here," Dream said, pacing back and forth.

"Strange like what?" Kay asked while cutting her steak.

"Zeke just passed out and Teresa is missing," Dream said.

"OK, let me figure something out. I will call you later," Kay said while feeding her dog a piece.

Teresa? I haven't heard that name in years. I've been so busy. I almost forgot how she just disappeared, Kay thought to herself while hitting her vape.

"Can you please bring the check?" Kay asked while also instructing the three beautiful ladies that sat in front of her to go grab the car.

"Make a left here," Kay said to Tokyo.

"Are you OK?" Paris asked Kay while putting $300,000 through a money counter.

"Yes, I'm OK. Just make sure your count is accurate," Kay said as she pulled out her cellular device.

"What's up, Kay Slay?" Carter asked while smoking on some of the finest cannabis money can buy.

"I need you to track a number," Kay demanded.

"Whose number?" Carter asked.

"Can you write down the numbers?" she asked.

"Read them to me," Carter replied while putting the cannabis on the ashtray that was located on the right side of his Mahogany desk.

"470-777-7777," Kay said while putting the counted money into her briefcase. "Once you track the last location of that number, I need you to pull the camera footage and let me know what you find."

"OK. Give me two hours," Carter said while putting the cannabis back to his full, black lips.

"Make it one hour," Kay instructed as she ended the call.

Kay knew she had to find out what had taken place—after all, the girl *did* save her life. She just wanted to know why she disappeared all of a sudden. When she put her head on the headrest, she started having flashbacks.

SOMEWHERE IN THE PAST—KAY'S FLASHBACK:

cough, cough

I have to find a way out of here, Kay thought as she made her way through the burning building.

Boom! Boom!

The guard shot at her, but missed because his vision was slightly compromised.

"Damn, that could have gone through my head," Kay said as she made a quick right through the burning building.

The smoke in the building was becoming unbearable, and everywhere Kay turned, it seemed like the building was getting hotter and hotter. The smoke choked her and burned her eyes, but she was trained and prepared for situations like this.

Boom! Boom!

"More gunshots," Kay said to herself while checking her clip.

Damn, three bullets left, she thought as she searched for her extra clip that was stashed away on her gun holsters.

Damn, it must've fell. She inhaled more smoke.

Who is that girl and why are these guys chasing her? Teresa thought to herself as sweat ran down her face.

Teresa knew she had to do something, and she would get the story about the mysterious woman later. The only thing on her mind was that she had to get the hell out of this burning building. Teresa crept behind the mysterious man; she then twisted his neck and put a bullet into his head.

I thought I lost them! Kay thought to herself.

"Ahhhhh!" Teresa screamed as a piece of the damaged ceiling fell onto her right leg.

Kay quickly stopped in her tracks as the screams of a woman alarmed her.

"Who the hell is that?" she asked herself aloud while the thick black smoke entered her lungs.

"Ahhhhhh!" screamed the mysterious woman as the floor that she lay on burned her skin.

Kay immediately looked back and saw a helpless woman. The woman reached out for help as tears fell down her face.

Should I leave her? Kay thought as the heat burned her eyes. Kay said a quick prayer, then turned back to help the mysterious woman.

"Thank you," Teresa said while Kay removed the broken ceiling from her leg.

"We have to find a way out of here," Teresa said as she limped down the hot, smoky and dangerous hallways.

"Why were those men after you?" Teresa asked.

"Never mind that! The real question is, why are you here?" Kay asked while fanning her burning eyes.

"I was here on a mission. You probably would be dead by now, had I not taken that guy out," Teresa said while she limped.

Kay looked back at her and knew that she was slowing them down. *What should I do with her?* Kay asked herself. "Let me help you," she told Teresa. "Put your arms around my neck. We don't have long. If we don't hurry, this building will cave in on us."

"I see an exit," said the injured Teresa.

"Ahhhhh!" they both screamed as the ceiling fell to the ground in the hallway next to them.

"This place is falling apart and the heat is becoming unbearable," Kay said while coughing.

"I can't breathe," Teresa said as she covered her nose and mouth.

BOOM! BOOM!

Kay kicked the exit door as hard as she could, but it wasn't budging. She knew she couldn't push the door with her hands because the door was too hot.

BOOM!

One last final kick and the door opened. The two of them looked at each other in disbelief as they disappeared down the stairs in hopes that the path was clear.

THE PRESENT:

I wonder… What's really going on? Kay thought to herself while closing her briefcase that held $1.5 million in it.

"Pull in the parking lot to your right and park by the yellow car on your right," Kay instructed Tokyo.

"P, you know what to do," Kay said.

When she handed Paris the suitcase, Paris exited the white luxury SUV with a cold-blooded mentality. She appeared to be gentle as a butterfly, but this was one butterfly who shouldn't be taken lightly. She immediately opened the trunk of the yellow vehicle, placed the briefcase inside, closed the trunk and joined the others in the white SUV.

"It's done," Paris said, never taking her eyes off the yellow SUV. Kay nodded while they disappeared into Miami's afternoon traffic.

SOMEWHERE IN A DARK, ABANDONED WAREHOUSE:

"Ughhhh," a groggy Teresa, awoke to the blunt blow from the butt of a gun. "What the hell is going on? And why can't I move?" she asked herself while trying to wiggle her way out of the uncomfortable chair. She scanned the dark and gloomy room."Where is Autumn? I need to find a way to get out of here."*My throat is really dry and it's hot in here,* she thought to herself while trying to swallow her saliva. Teresa's sudden movements alerted one of the nearby guards. He walked into the room wearing a goat head mask, and in his hands he carried a shotgun that was fully loaded. The powerful footsteps alerted Teresa. She knew that something, or someone, was coming her way, and that they had a raging spirit.

"I think this one is awake. Hit the lights!" demanded the guard! When the lights came on, Teresa tried her best to make out the mysterious figure, but her vision was slightly compromised.

She shook her head from left to right in hopes that the room would stop spinning. When she made out the person who was standing in front of her, it brought chills to her soul.

"Ahhhhhhhhh!" Teresa let out a muffled scream.

The guard standing in front of her let out the evilest laugh as Teresa tried to scream through the duct tape.

"What's wrong, beautiful? You've never seen a goat-head before?" asked the guard while he ripped the duct tape from her mouth. Teresa screamed to the top of her lungs; as the duct tape was ripped off her full lips, it felt like her lips came off with it.

The sounds of her pain gave the guards an adrenaline rush and it also fueled their egos.

"What the hell do you guys want with me? Where is Autumn?!" Teresa asked.

"She's right over there," said the guard who stood behind her.

Teresa slowly turned her head as she prepared for the worst. She was petrified when she witnessed Autumn bonded, gagged and still asleep.

"What the hell did you do to her?" Teresa yelled while attempting to break free from her chair once again.

"She's a feisty one," said the guard while injecting a syringe into Autumn's left arm.

Autumn was slowly awakened by the fluids that were injected into her arm. She felt lost, confused and scared.

"What are you doing? Get away from her!" Teresa screamed.

When she yelled at the beast, one of them walked towards her with such force that she could feel a slight breeze as he passed. The guard backhanded Teresa with such a vengeful hand that it almost snapped her neck.

"WWWHHHYYY?!" she yelled.

The blow she endured made her dizzy, which disabled her eyesight. She felt like she had just been hit by a ton of bricks. Her face tingled and burned, and her head was pounding. He must've split something inside of Teresa's mouth because she felt blood leaking out of her mouth uncontrollably.

"Huh… huh? What's going on? I feel so weak and lightheaded. Why can't I move? Where am I?" Autumn mumbled while trying to regain her composure.

"Autumn, are you OK?!" Teresa yelled.

"I thought I told you to shut up!" yelled a guard.

"Ahhhhhhhh!" Teresa screamed.

The guard hit her in the right eye with such vengeance that blood instantly began to leak from it uncontrollably, making it even harder for her to see.

The tranquilizers that Autumn was waking up from quickly wore off as she watched a guard hit Teresa in the face.

"Ahhhhhhhh!" Autumn screamed.

She couldn't bear to watch the once-beautiful Teresa being treated like a punching bag. The situation brought horror into Autumn's soul. Her thoughts were interrupted by a pair of soulless hands. The guard squeezed Autumn's throat with so much pressure that it cut her air supply.

"Shut the hell up! Nobody gave you permission to speak!" said the evil guard.

After he removed his hands from around her neck, Autumn struggled to inhale as the guard left visible handprints around her soft, milky skin.

"If I ever get free… all you bastards are deaaaddd!!!" Teresa yelled, attempting to wiggle her hands out of the tight ropes that were cutting off her blood circulation.

"Lady, you will never make it out of here alive!" a mysterious voice said. The room erupted into laughter.

Autumn tried to focus on her surroundings, but the evil laughter made her teeth chatter.

Oh, my God! Are these guys wearing masks, or do they really have goat heads? I don't understand. Are these Mr. Henderson's guards? Autumn asked herself while she continued to scan the old, smelly building.

What she saw was that all the guards had goat heads with pentagram stamped on their forehead. The old building was dark, gloomy, rusted and filled with a foul smell. Butterflies began to turn within her stomach and chills shot down her spine as she tried to wiggle her way out of the chair.

"What kind of sick shit are you guys on?" Autumn asks.

"You haven't seen sick yet," one of the guards replied vengefully.

"If you guys are going to kill us, then do it now," Teresa said.

"Oh, we are not going to kill you," a whisper from the back of the room said.

"Then, what the hell do you want with us?" Teresa asked.

"Your souls," said the mysterious voice in the back of the dark and gloomy room.

''Are you fucking kidding me?" said both of the women in disbelief.

As the sound of the machine cut on, a gentleman's voice sprung from the back of the room. "You guys can get started now."

The chill of fear rushed throughout their bodies as they had not a clue what was about to take place. Autumn continued to panic as she tried to move the chair she was sitting in, but couldn't.

Fuck. The chair is bolted to the ground, she thought to herself in panic.

"If it's money you're after, I can pay you whatever you want! Name the price!" Autumn yelled as beads of sweat flowed down her face.

The guards started to chant a demonic song like they were getting ready for a marathon. As the chanting took place, two guards approached Autumn with machetes in their hands.

"Nobody told you to speak," one of the guards said as he chopped off her right pinky finger.

The pain she felt was like no other; this knife just cut through her flesh and bone like butter. When she looked down and saw her pinky missing and the amount of blood that leaked from where it once was, she pissed on herself as tears flooded her eyes. She was beginning to go into shock.

"Ahhhhhhhh! Please don't! *Please* don't!" Autumn begged.

One of the guards ripped Autumn's blouse open, revealing her breasts. This made her scream even louder as tears continued to flow from her puffy eyes. Fear dwelt within the cores of her shaking body. The guard pulled out a pair of scissors and cut off all of Autumn's hair.

The other guard put on a pair of brass knuckles. "OOF!!!" With one punch, he broke Autumn›s lower ribs.

"Ahhhhhhhh!!" Autumn screamed.

At that moment, she wished she was dead.

"Leave her alone!!!" Teresa yelled. Before she could let out another word, a guard used a nail gun and put three nails into her kneecap. Her cries and screams were so loud and painful that they could have awoken the dead.

"Why are you guys doing this?!" Autumn screamed.

"Hey, wait your turn! And didn't I tell you to speak only when spoken to?!" the guard shouted. He then aimed the nail gun at Autumn and shot four nails into her left foot.

The guards were so distracted by Autumn's agony and pain that they hadn't realized Teresa had broken free and was now out of her chair. She looked Autumn in the eyes and put her index finger to her lips, signaling her to keep quiet. Teresa crept behind a guard who was enjoying Autumn screams and cries. She reached for his shotgun, but was quickly apprehended.

"Hey! What do you think you're doing, little lady?" asked a guard while another guard pepper-sprayed her right in the eyes.

"This one's a fighter. I love fighters. Now, bring me the meat hooks!" demanded the guard.

Once one of the guard's henchmen brought out the meat hooks, two guards instantly tied Teresa's wrists to the meat hooks, pulled her feet off the ground and stripped her naked.

As Autumn watched in horror, drool dripped from her mouth. Her broken lower rib was making it harder and harder for her to breathe.

"God, please help us." Autumn said a silent prayer, as her body began to shiver and shake.

Hanging from the meat hooks, the young Teresa's eyes continued to burn from the pepper spray. The ropes were cutting into her wrist and she began to think to herself, *Could this be a retaliation from the Russians for killing Helga? This is all my fault!* Her thoughts were interrupted by the pain and the sounds of her very own flesh being ripped by a thick, rusted chain.

"Ahhhhhhhh!" Teresa let out an excruciating scream.

When the chain fell off her skin, parts of her flesh and bones went with it. Autumn watched in horror at the torture and humiliation being inflicted on Teresa. One of the guards caught her by surprise. He grabbed Autumn by the jaw, then used a pair of pliers to rip four teeth out of her mouth.

"MMMMMM… AHHHHHH!!!" Autumn screamed, but the blood erupting in her mouth made it sound muffled.

Tension, as well as revenge, crept through the air as the guards enjoyed the infliction of never-ending pain upon the two helpless women. The room was engulfed with screams and evil laughter as another guard began to rip Autumn's nails off one by one. Autumn wanted to pass out, as the pain was unbearable, but the substance that was used to awaken her also forced her body to stay awake.

"You guys have fun and call me when you are done," said a mysterious voice from the back of the room. The entire time this anonymous person spoke, nobody seemed to see who he was, not even the guards. It was as if he was sent here by Lucifer himself.

"Yyyooouuu eeevvviiilll mooothhherrr fuccckkkeeerrr!" yelled Teresa.

Three demonic guards quickly approached Teresa and gave her blows to the ribs and stomach while she hung like a piece of meat. Autumn faded in and out and was fully awakened by a sledgehammer to the knees. This sent instant shock waves through her body. She coughed and cried with the most traumatic voices that could be heard, but sadly, none of them were. Autumn caught left and right hooks to the face with brass knuckles, which dislocated her jawbone.

"Hey, lower that rope!" demanded one of the henchmen.

In the process, Teresa got three more whacks with the thick chain. More of her flesh continued ripping as her blood spewed into the air. At this time, Teresa began to say a prayer to God as an apology for her part in all her negative things, especially her dealings with Helga. "Maybe I was wrong about her, dear Lord," she said quietly.

Another henchman broke Autumn›s left arm. Autumn instantly collapsed in the chair and was awakened once more, this time by a bucket of scalding hot water, giving parts of her body third-degree burns.

"Ahhhhhhhh! Help us, sssooommmeeebbbooodddyyy!!!" Autumn screamed and begged.

"Why does she still have on clothes?" asked a demonic henchman with an evil smile.

The other henchman began to strip Autumn naked, revealing all of her bruises, scars, open flesh wounds and broken bones. Teresa lay on her stomach while two guards held her down with excessive force. Another henchman carved a pentagram in the middle of her back with a dull, rusty knife. Teresa screamed with such pain as the men boldly laughed and made fun of her.

"Look at the little bad bitch now! You scream as if it hurts, and it doesn't," said the henchman as another guard walked over to her with a bottle of pure alcohol.

This was more than she could bear. Teresa continued to yell and scream louder and louder as the dull knife pierced her back.

While she screamed and squirmed like a fish, the henchman poured 100 percent alcohol all over Teresa's body. The same demonic henchman walked over to Autumn and began to carve a pentagram into her stomach with the same rusty knife he had used on Teresa.

"Bone of bone and flesh of flesh," said the henchman as he licked the blood from the knife.

Autumn instantly threw up in his face, and out of rage, he stabbed her in the stomach. Blood instantly gushed out of her mouth. With the old rusty knife piercing her stomach, she went into instant shock as she choked on her own blood and began to say her last and final prayers. Autumn knew this would be her end; she felt as if all of her past demons had just finally caught up with her.

"Hey! Bring me the center block!" a henchman requested.

"Fuck you, motherfucker! Fffuuuccckkk yyyooouuu!" yelled Teresa.

A straight kick to the face broke Teresa's nose and four of her teeth. Her body went completely limp as she lay naked on the cold, bloody floor. As blood continued to run from her broken nose and mouth like waterfalls in the Himalayan mountains, she was suddenly awoken by the sharp pains of a sledgehammer breaking both of her ankles! The screams Teresa let out could have been heard from a mile away. The pain that was being inflicted on these women was giving the henchmen a rush. It was as if they were receiving unwanted power and feeding off the ladies' unwanted fear!

"Someone put something in that bitch's mouth!" demanded a henchman. "Oh, *I* have something to put in her mouth," another henchman replied.

When Teresa heard belts unloosen and pants unzipping, she closed her eyes and prepared for the worst. She knew that anything was possible at this moment, even being raped. The guards and henchmen had no remorse; it was clear that these guys were pros and had done this many times before.

One of the henchmen grabbed her by the hair and said, "Naw! This one is a biter!"

"I'm pretty sure this one can't bite. She has no jaw," said the other henchman while gagging Autumn with his 10 inches.

Autumn watched helplessly as two other demonic henchmen pinned Teresa down. Tears flooded Autumn's eyes at the sight of Teresa being raped and beaten. At that point in time, Autumn knew what she had been smelling. The whole entire time, they both were being introduced to death!

"Untie her from that chair!" yelled one of the henchmen.

Autumn wanted to fight, but she had no fight left in her. The girls realized that if they didn't pull their heads together and fast, then there wouldn't be a tomorrow for them. It was plain and simple to see that these guys would not stop until both of them were dead.

Teresa began to think, focusing on all the strength she had left in hopes that she could make one last attempt to escape.

If we don't do something right now, these things are going to kill us! I need to communicate with Autumn somehow! She thought to herself as a guard poured bleach on her naked, bruised, cut and slaughtered body.

"Ahhhhhhhh!" she screamed.

When the bleach touched her open flesh wounds, it felt like pure acid. She could feel the bleach entering each and every single cut. It burned her eyes, it burned her ribs, it burned her spine. The guard didn't stop pouring until the entire bottle was empty.

Teresa looked over to her left and watched helplessly while Autumn was being raped and tortured…

"Noooooooo!" a muffled scream came out of Autumn's mouth while another guard punched her in the face repeatedly.

Tears rolled down Teresa's swollen face and she wanted to scream. The pain was super unbearable; a guard had just punched her in the left eye and it felt as if her eyeball came out of its socket. Her vision was flooded with blood, stars and a mob of angry demonic, goat-headed henchmen.

"Autumn, please focus, because if you don't, we are going to die here! There is still a future for us. We *can't* let them win. I know you can hear me," Teresa said using telepathic waves.

Although Autumn was extremely injured, she could have sworn she heard Teresa's voice, but when she looked over to her right, she watched helplessly as a demonic guard poured bleach all over Teresa's body. Autumn closed her eyes and began to hear Teresa's voice again.

"Autumn, it's me, Teresa. If you can hear me, please focus. I know you have the gift."

"Teresa, how are we… and when did you…?" Autumn asked in confusion using telepathic waves.

"Autumn, listen. We have to get away. Please focus. If you don't, we are going to die here."

Autumn closed her eyes and mustered all the energy she had left. She also felt a powerful source of energy illuminating off Teresa's wounded body. In the next second, it was as if time itself stood still, and all of Autumn's pains and hurt stopped. She could no longer hear Teresa's screams or cries. They both felt a sense of peace.

"Are we in heaven?" Autumn asked using telepathic waves.

"No, we are not dead! I need you to use that energy you feel," Teresa replied. Autumn knew that it was up to her to rescue the both of them. Teresa had kept her from losing it, and now, it was her time to bring them the rest of the way. The demonic guards stopped all movements and unwanted activities and stood at attention. They had been hit by a phenomenal and powerful wave of unknown energy and were now being controlled by the two badly injured women. The demonic henchmen were so hypnotized that if someone were to snap their fingers in front of their faces, they wouldn't blink or move not one muscle. All the henchmen pulled their pants up, grabbed a gun of their choice and put the barrels of the weapons inside their mouths.

BOOOOM!

All five demonic guards fell to their knees and collapsed onto the cold, bloody floor. Autumn's eyes grew extremely big and she wanted to smile, but she was fading in and out of consciousness.

"Autumn, I don't have a lot of energy left; we need each other's energies to finish the job. Is everyone dead?" Teresa asked using telepathic waves.

"There's no one left here. I've scanned the whole room and we're the only ones living," Autumn responded.

"We are in no shape to walk! We have to use our minds to travel outside of this room. Close your eyes and focus," Teresa instructed, now using telepathic waves to accomplish their mission.

Together, they found a homeless man five miles down the road. When he awoke from his nap, the man jumped up and started walking down the street like a zombie. He was no longer in control of his body; instead, the girls were leading him straight to them. They were driving him like an old 1979 Geo with a bad oil leak and a power steering pump that went bad two months ago and was in need of a serious tune-up. The homeless man walked through the gates of the old, abandoned building; it smelled like dead bodies, rotten flesh and hot garbage. He looked down and saw five beasts lying on the floor with their brains painted all over the walls.

"Hey, you! Help us, please! Help us!" yelled Teresa.

Autumn couldn›t hold on any longer and she began to black out. She felt peace and tranquility at that moment, a feeling that reminded her of Christmas morning, so she let her mind, body and soul drift over as she went into the light.

"Autumn!!! Autumn!!! Please hold on!" Teresa cried. Sir, grab my cell phone out that purse over there. The code is 2007. Please call the police!" yelled the badly injured Teresa.

The old man quickly grabbed the cell phone and dialed 911…

"Autumn, help is on the way!" Teresa yelled, but watched as Autumn's body went completely limp…

"Ma'am!!! The police are on their way!" yelled the old man.

Teresa tried to hold on as long as she could, but slowly, she went out cold…

"HUH?" Autumn said to herself as she was awoken by a sharp blade cutting into her skin.

She felt no pain. She had no emotions regarding the situation and the only thing she wanted was peace. She wanted to just die! *Why haven't they killed us yet?* she thought to herself in disappointment.

"Oh, no," she said as she watched Teresa laying on the cold and bloody floor.

The two women were still in the old warehouse. They never escaped and both of them felt like they were doomed! Autumn must've fallen asleep somehow during the torture and pain. The tranquilizers that were pumping through her veins must've had her hallucinating. Autumn quickly closed her eyes, hoping that Teresa would hear her and they could attempt to escape once again.

What the hell is going on?! Kay thought as she, Paris and Tokyo loaded their weapons.

"Why is that unmarked vehicle parked outside?" Paris asked while loading some explosives into her duffle bag.

"Are you sure this is the right address?" Tokyo asked.

"Y'all know Carter isn't going to send me on a dummy mission," Kay said while examining the evidence Carter gave her.

She looked through several photos and watched as two gentlemen escorted Teresa and some other girls to an all-black SUV. She looked to her left and spotted the same SUV parked in the old, abandoned warehouse parking lot. *Whose unmarked vehicle is this?* she thought to herself while taking a closer look at the evidence.

"What does this look like to you, P?" Kay asked as she handed Paris some photos.

"It looks like the Feds, and that's the same vehicle that's parked right over there," Paris said while handing Tokyo some photos.

"What should we do?" Tokyo asked.

"I'm not trying to get caught in a shootout with the Feds! if we were getting paid, then I would consider it, but this is a favor for a friend," Kay said while smoking a -flavored vape.

"Let's see what the Feds got up their sleeves before we make any moves," she said, then called Carter for further information.

"Who's driving that SUV that is parking behind us?" Samantha asked while loading her golden guns.

"I don't know. Maybe I should go check it out," said Agent Dixon as he finished the rest of his coffee.

"Hey! If anything looks suspicious, light that motherfucker up," said Samantha.

"I'll save my ammunition for the real bad guys," he replied.

"How do you know… that they are not the bad guys?" Samantha asked.

"I just have a good feeling," said Agent Dixon while exiting the unmarked car.

"There's one of your Feds," said Tokyo while pulling the hammer back on her nine-millimeter.

"No, Tokyo! We're not killing a federal agent. Just be cool," demanded Kay Slay.

"Hey! My name is CIA Agent Dixon. Please move your SUV *now*! This area is restricted," he instructed while flashing his credentials.

"Move the vehicle, Tokyo!" Paris said while typing in CIA Agent Dixon's credentials. "Oh! He's fine *and* Jamaican," she said as she did further research.

"P! How do you know that officer is Jamaican?" Kay asked while Tokyo exited the old warehouse parking lot.

"Heehee!" Paris chuckled very seductively.

"It was just a bunch of kids," said Agent Dixon while entering the unmarked SUV.

"OK! Now that you're done babysitting, are you ready to play hero?" Samantha asked.

"I'm ready to do my job! The reason I signed up to be a CIA agent was to take out these bumbaclots," he said in his Jamaican accent.

"Save the speech for Election Day," Samantha said while exiting the unmarked SUV.

"It smells like death in here," agent Dixon said.

"It smells like a whole lot of cash and a big promotion for the both of us," Samantha said very devilishly.

Agent Dixon watched, dissected and studied the way Samantha walked through the old, dusty, gloomy and dark warehouse like she was the queen of this unholy dungeon. *It looks like she's been here before. This is very familiar territory for Samantha,* Agent Dixon thought to himself very suspiciously.

"Samantha, where are we going?" he asked.

"Just follow me," she said.

"How do you know the way?" he asked very suspiciously.

"Stop asking all these questions! Don't you wanna be rich?" she asked while turning around and looking Officer Dixon in his face.

This time when he looked into her eyes, he saw greed and the true Samantha. He saw the demon within her, and Agent Dixon finally knew who he was dealing with. She looked like she had just hit some serious drugs; her eyes were bulging out of her head and her hair looked stringy as sweat ran down her face.

"What's wrong ,Samantha?" he asked.

"Listen! This could be a big deal! Picture this: two CIA agents coming in to save two beautiful Black girls from the hands of the most dangerous man on the planet."

"What are you planning?" Dixon asked.

"Are you in or out?" Samantha asked while pointing a gun at Agent Dixon's head.

"Samantha, that's the last time you will point a gun in my face," he said while reaching for his nine-millimeter.

"Go ahead! I will blow you away before you pull the trigger," she said with lots of confidence.

"Put the gun down, Samantha!" Kay said as she, Tokyo and Paris pointed infrared beams at Samantha's forehead.

"Ahhhhhhhh! No! Please stop!" yelled a mysterious woman.

Suddenly, everybody in the room except for Samantha turned their heads in the direction where the screams were coming from.

Boom!

Samantha shot Agent Dixon in the left leg and tried to make a quick getaway.

"Uggghhh! You fucker, you!" Agent Dixon grunted while ripping his T- Shirt and applying pressure to his open gunshot wound.

"Don't take another step, Samantha," Kay Slay said.

" Who are you?" Samantha asked, her face full of suspicion.

"The one who will send you to your grave if you don't run me the $1.4 billion you owe me," Kay said while signaling Paris and Tokyo to go help Teresa. Kay Slay knew those screams from anywhere.

I hope she's alright; those were the same screams I heard when I first met her, Kay Slay thought to herself as chills ran down her spin.

"I owe you $1.4 billion? Hahahaha!" Samantha chuckled.

"You stole money out of 100 of my accounts and more money out of 200 accounts that were owned by two of my business associates over a period of seven months. That shit added up."

"Why would you allow someone to keep stealing from you?" Samantha asked.

"'Cause I wanted to see who was stupid enough to fuck with me," Kay said, gripping her trigger a little harder.

"I don't steal! I'm CIA!" Samantha barked.

"No! You didn't steal anything, your den of thieves did! The ones you have on a private unmarked island somewhere overseas. That's where you Feds keep your rats at!" Kay said while Agent Dixon recorded Everything.

Samantha took a closer look at the women standing in front of her. She was about five feet, five inches tall. She wore all black, her hair was long and golden and she had an hourglass shape. She wore an all-expensive genuine leather black catsuit with a pair of designer kitten-heeled boots. Her skin was bright like a winter morning, and she was extremely beautiful.

"It's sad that all that beauty is about to fade. Once I..."

BOOM!

Samantha was interrupted by Kay's bullet piercing her forehead.

"I don't have time for all that talking," Kay said while pulling Samantha's device out of her pocket.

Agent Dixon's mouth was wide open during the entire conversation; he was shocked that Samantha had been utilizing CIA resources to make billions of dollars. He recorded the entire conversation while he watched in suspense. Dixon knew Samantha was a dirty cop, but he didn't know how dirty she actually was. Samantha was filthier than a chicken coop that hadn't been cleaned in eons.

"I would blow your ass away, too, but my people got plans for you! So, you can live for now," Kay said, then ran to join the others.

"Shit! I better call for backup," Agent Dixon said while looking at

Samantha's lifeless corpse.

"This is Agent Dixon! We got an officer down and one wounded. I need backup," Agent Dixon said as he searched for the first aid kit.

"Who were those three women? And what did the young woman, Kay, mean when she said, 'My people have plans for you'? And who was the other girl who ran off with the other young lady? She looked at me like she wanted to take my clothes off," he said to himself while cleaning his gunshot wounds in the unmarked vehicle.

"Fuck you, motherfucker! Fffuuuccckkk yyyooouuu!" yelled Teresa.

A straight kick to the face brakes Teresa's nose and sent four teeth straight into her mouth. Her body went completely limp as she lay naked on the cold and bloody floor. As blood continued to run from her broken nose and mouth like waterfalls from the Himalayan mountains, she was suddenly awoken by the sharp pains of a sledgehammer breaking both of her ankles! The screams Teresa let out could have been heard from a mile away. The pain that was being inflicted on these women was giving the henchmen a rush. It was as if they were receiving unwanted power and feeding off the two ladies' unwanted fear!

"What is happening here?" Tokyo asked while holding her nose.

"I don't know, but this is some sick shit! But why are they being tortured like this?" Paris asked with pleading eyes.

"Where's Kay?" Tokyo asked while pulling the hammer back on her nine-millimeter.

"I don't know!" Paris replied as she aimed her weapons at one of the goat-headed guards.

Autumn saw an infrared beam shining. She didn't know to feel scared or happy, but something told her that faith was on her and Teresa's side.

"Hey!!! Stupid!!! Leave her alone!" Autumn yelled, trying to distract the guards from seeing the infrared beams, but she sounded like she had just gotten all her wisdom teeth removed at the dentist.

"What does Autumn have up her sleeve?" Teresa asked herself. She tried to make out Autumn's face, but the blood and chemicals that lingered impaired her vision.

Boom!

A clean shot to the head laid out one of the guards who was on top of Teresa.

"What the fuck was that?!" Teresa asked herself in shock.

Boom! Boom!

Two more guards were instantly taken out by Tokyo's sharp shooting skills.

Oh, thank you, God! That's gotta be Zeke coming to save me, thought the badly injured Autumn.

"Zeke, I'm over here," said Autumn using telepathic waves.

Damnit! More gunshots! I hope I'm not too late! thought Kay as she ran like the wind to help the others. Beads of sweat ran down her face; the warehouse was hot and dark. She heard screams and gunshots, but didn't know which way to go.

Who the hell are these ladies? thought a henchman while ducking behind an old, rusty pillar.

"Ahhhh! Fuck!" shouted Tokyo as a bullet grazed her arm and disabled her weapons.

"TOKYO! Are you OK?!" screamed Paris.

"I'm fine! It's just a flesh wound! What happened to my gun?" asked Tokyo while applying pressure to her wound.

"Ahhhhhh! Please get off me!" yelled Autumn.

Boom! A clean shot to the head splattered the guard's brains onto Autumn's face.

"Got you, motherfucker!" said the badly injured Teresa in a raspy voice.

"Tokyo, are you OK?" Said Kay while ripping a piece of Tokyo's shirt off and wrapping up her wounds.

Boom! Boom! Boom! Boom! Boom!

Five clean shots from kay's gun took out the rest of the guards in the building.

The room got completely silent and everybody looked at everybody. Kay and Paris examined their bodies to make sure they weren't hit.

"Let's get the fuck out of here!" said Tokyo.

"Yeah, there's one dead officer and one is wounded. This place will be covered with Feds," said Kay, then she walked over to help Teresa.

"K… how did you find me?" asked the badly injured Teresa.

"Never mind that. We have to move you and get you some type of help immediately!" Kay said with a hint of panic in her voice.

"Kay! Listen, we have to go; the police are about to surround this place. Let the professionals save them! We don't have the manpower," said Paris while helping Tokyo to her feet.

"She's right, Kay, and that Fed you shot is not a good look," said Tokyo as she held her flesh wound.

"I can't just leave them!" Kay said.

"The ambulance is on the way. I just sent an anonymous tip! Listen, they can do more for them than we can," Paris said.

"You're right," Kay responded.

"Listen! Teresa, the ambulance is on their way. I will make sure you get to the hospital safely," said Kay, then she and the two other ladies disappeared into the dark, evil and gloomy warehouse.

Autumn and Teresa looked at the women leave and all hope was regained, but also lost because they both were losing lots of blood and their internal organs were shutting down.

"I can't… " were the last words Autumn whispered.

"Hold on, Autumn! Help is on the way," Teresa whispered as she faded into the unknown depths of unconsciousness.

"Are you OK?" an officer asked Dixon.

"Yes, I'm well! Did you find Samantha?" he asked.

"We searched the warehouse. The only things we found were two girls and a bunch of weird guys with goat masks. Why were they torturing those two women?" the redheaded officer asked.

"I don't know why you guys can't locate Samantha,. I watched her get shot when she was there," Agent Dixon said while being carried away on a stretcher and loaded into the back of an ambulance.

"So, what's the deal with him?" asked a fat, lazy Cop.

"I don't know, but there's one hell of a story here," said the redheaded officer.

This is WDCKI Action News. Hi, I'm Diane, and we're live at the crime scene where an officer almost lost his life in pursuit to save two women. CIA Agent Dixon is truly a hero. We haven't received an update on his current condition, but from what I heard, he suffers from a bullet wound to the leg. The current conditions of the two women are still unknown. Tom, I'm here, and it is a very horrifying and sad situation. As you can see here, several CIA and FBI agents have the entire intersection blocked off. So, be on the lookout for a major traffic jam. The search for a missing federal agent is still underway and several dead bodies have just been found inside the same old, abandoned warehouse! I will have a better update a little later. For now, it's back to you, Tom.

Paris, Kay and Tokyo sat back and laughed evilly as they watched Samantha's plans crumble right before their sleepy eyes.

"Hey! She passed out again. I'm dying to use this artificial adrenaline that I found inside the old warehouse," said Paris while injecting the syringe inside the vial containing the artificial adrenaline.

"No, I need her fully rested. Let's stick to the plan! Get the cash first. Then, you can have as much fun as you'd like with her, Dr. Paris," said Kay very evilly.

BOOM!

A loud explosion that sent the warehouse into flames minutes ago has Killed three officers and injured many! Firefighters are still trying to contain the fires from the mysterious explosion. Nobody knows what actually caused the old warehouse to shoot up in flames. Investigators say it could've been an old gas leak; we should have an update soon. Right now, many officers are fighting for their lives while several medics tend to the injured and wounded officers! This has truly been one heck of a nightmare! Back to you, Just'n.

"Yes, hi! Diane, are you OK out there?" Just'n asked.

"Yes. My current conditions are stable. It's a little hard to breathe with all the smoke in the air, and just seeing all these injured officers has truly been one heck of an experience."

"Did you speak to any of the officers before the massive explosion?" Just'n asked.

"Yes. I interviewed several officers before the explosion. We will have exclusive footage later at 10 p.m.," Diane said while staring into the camera.

"What about Agent Dixon? Are there any updates on his current condition?" Just'n asked in shock.

"Agent Dixon's current condition is stable, but he chooses not to speak about any of the tragic events that took place tonight," she said.

"Alright, Diane. Stay safe and we will be back at 10 p.m.," Just'n said, then ended the broadcast.

"You guys will never make it out of here alive," Samantha said, then passed out cold.

"Let me finish this bitch off. And this time, we won't miss," said Paris as she pointed a gun to Samantha's temple.

"Let's just wait another hour or two. In the meantime, I need you to hack into these accounts and locate the money," Kay instructed while puffing her-flavored vape.

BACK AT THE NEWS STATION:

"Just'n, we have reports that Samantha is still alive," said the private eye.

"Find her! Don't eat, don't sleep, don't even take a sip of water until you have her exact location."

"OK," said the private eye while leaving Just'n's office nervously.

"Samantha, you sneaky little cunt! I will have your head," said Just'n to himself vengefully.

Knock, knock!

"Come in," said Just'n.

"Hey, you're on in 10 minutes," said Just'n's assistant.

"Thank you! I will be out shortly," he replied as he slowly sipped his pine needle tea.

Throughout the torture, agony and pain, Teresa , being as strong-minded and determined as she was, somehow continued her struggle. As she guided herself and Autumn throughout this tragedy, it remained as if it was all a part of her plan. This will enable, as well as strengthen, the both of them to overcome their pain and suffering.

You see, Autumn, whether she realized it or not, was in debt to Teresa for life—she's the reason the both of them remained alive. To overcome the alpha and the omega was truly one extraordinary experience.

UNPLUG YOURSELF FROM THE MATRIX!

CHAPTER 5
VIP ACCESS

Two Days Later:

Beep... beeeppp... beeeppp!

Zeke quickly woke up to the sounds of a heart monitor, and as the beeping sounds got louder, his heart rate began to speed up. His vision was blurred and his head was pounding. Zeke felt like his body weighed a thousand pounds. He felt lost and hopeless, not to mention his heart felt as if it was jumping out of his chest. He began to see quick flashes of a woman who was in serious danger.

At, the time he didn't know who she was or what would cause this to happen, especially now. Blood began to pour from his nose and his body started to shake uncontrollably.

"Zeke!!! It's me, your mother. You are safe. Please calm down!" she yelled.

Instantly, his heart rate began to slow down. Zeke tried to focus on what was going on, but his vision was slightly blurred. He knew that he needed some time to get things back in perspective. After he focused on his surroundings, Zeke's vision became clear and his mother was standing over him with the biggest smile on her beautiful little face. It was like a breath of fresh air to Zeke.

"Hey, son. I'm glad to see that you have awakened," said his mother with lots of excitement in her voice.

"Hello, Zeke! My name is Dr. Williams. How are you feeling?" she asked while holding a small flashlight to Zeke's eyes.

"How many fingers am I holding up?" Dr. Williams asked in concern.

"Three," Zeke replied very dryly.

"He is going to be just fine. He does suffer from neuroplasticity, however," said the doctor with lots of confidence in her craft.

Mother looked at Dr. Williams with a face of confusion. "Smaller words, please!" Zeke's mother replied.

"It simply means he suffers from some type of trauma."

"Doc, can you please give us a moment?" Zeke's mother asked while scratching her head.

"Yes, ma'am! Take as long as you need. Just press the red button over there if you need anything." The doctor quickly put the flashlight back into the pocket of her all-white lab coat and signed the log sheet on the wall. Once Dr. Williams exited the room, Zeke's mother looked at him with eyes that held pain, hurt and misery.

"Mom! Teresa is in danger... I had a crazy dream."

"ZEKE! STOP! Save your energy. I need you to listen to me very carefully. You have been in a coma for two days." Zeke's eyes grew extremely big; this news just came in like a wrecking ball to him. "Now, what I'm about to tell you may be very disturbing! But I need you to keep calm because this is my third attempt to tell you this story. Every time I get halfway through it, you pass out. Now that I have your attention, would you please focus? Here, take a sip of this cold water," his mother said, frustrated.

Zeke drank the ice cold water like a madman who had not had anything to drink in several days.

"Zeke, Teresa has been raped and beaten very badly. Several bones have been broken, as well. Somebody tortured her almost to death."

Zeke's eyes begin to roll to the back of his head. The news he was receiving triggered the screams and cries he heard in his dream.

"Who is the other girl with Teresa? I can't make out their faces..." Zeke's said to himself while slipping into another coma.

Still a bit faded, Zeke didn't have the slightest idea of Autumn's danger, but was about to find out very quickly. As quick flashes continued to flood his vision, the young Zeke held on to all the strength he had left.

"It was Autumn!" he said loudly.

He watched in horror as several men beat them senseless. They even carved pentagrams into their stomachs and backs. Suddenly, all the pain and suffering that they endured fell upon Zeke.

"Oh, no! Not this again. I'm not losing him this time," his mother said with lots of determination and love.

Zeke was quickly awoken by a nice splash of hot water to the face.

"What the hell, Mom?!"

"Now, you listen to me, mister! I *need* you to stay awake!" yelled his mother.

The doctors and nurses quickly entered the room due to the commotion.

"Is everything alright? "asked the doctor with a voice of concern.

"Yes, everything is fine. He just spilled a little water trying to pick his cup up," mother replied with a fake smile.

The doctors and nurses shook their heads and slowly exited the room. Zeke's mother quickly continued her conversation after the room was safe from prying ears.

"However! Autumn was involved, too. There is no trace of her." This news was very disturbing to the half-awake Zeke!

"I tried to get in touch with her stepmother, but allegedly, she's missing, too. Also, all their numbers have been disconnected, not to mention Teresa is going to have to go under some major surgery. When the police found them, they were shocked that your sister and Autumn were still alive. Do you have any idea of who could have done such a terrible thing?"

"No ma'am, but when I find out…" Zeke said, attempting to make a fist.

"Hold on! Zeke, there it is."

His mother quickly grabbed the hospital remote and turned up the small plasma TV that hung on the wall.

This is WDCKI Action News and I'm Diane. We are live on the scene where two women were found. Their conditions are severe! The two young women were beaten almost to death. The families and local authorities suggested that their identities remain unknown. The FBI and other authorities have taken over this case. There are no leads just yet, but they also discovered five more unidentified bodies inside the old warehouse!

Zeke then turned the TV off and said, "Mom, please stop with the news..."

As said best by a great, powerful and talented artist, the number one rule on this earth is to never pay attention to anything you hear or see on the news.

"Can you please give me a second, Mom? I need to take all of this in," said Zeke.

" Sure thing. And your father has been asking about you," she said while closing the door behind her.

When Zeke closed his eyes, he started searching for any clue that would help crack this unsolved mystery. He was immediately disturbed by the sounds of his cell phone...

RING! RING! RING!

"Hello?" Zeke answered.

"Heeeyyy! Zeke, you sound like you had a wild and crazy night. Are you hungover?"

"No, I'm not feeling too well," Zeke lied.

" Kemi and I thought you had got picked up by the Feds! We've been trying to reach you, but anyways, it's good to hear from you! The reason I called was because I wanted to know if you were in Florida," Miami asked.

"Naw, I'm not. Why? What's up?" Zeke asked in suspicion.

"Too bad, because a friend of mine is having a big yacht party this weekend!"

"I'm going through something, so I'm not gonna be able to make it," Zeke replied very bluntly.

"Yo' boi has been down here for the last couple of weeks. So, I kinda figured you would have been here, as well," said Miami while having a sip of her margarita on the rocks.

Right now, there's so much drama going on that I don't know if I can really trust Miami. She sounds like she may be up to something, he thought.

"Diego has been in Florida? With who?" Zeke asked in confusion.

"He's down here with Kemi! They have been balling and living it up," Miami said abruptly.

For some odd reason, Zeke felt as if things were not stable and something was up, but he couldn't quite put the pieces to the puzzles together yet.

"They just came back from a seven-day cruise and stopped in Puerto Rico to go ring shopping." Miami explained.

"Why hasn't Kemi called me? That seems pretty weird!" Zeke asked Miami very dryly.

"Yeah, that *is* weird! Well, if you feel any better…"

Zeke quickly interrupted Miami and said, "I will try to make it."

"OK... well, TTYL, and you make sure you get better," Miami said as she ended the call.

Diego is in Miami, Florida with Kemi. All of this seems a bit too strange. Let me give her a ring. He called Kemi.

Hi! You have reached Kemi. I'm sorry, I can't come to my phone right now. Please leave your message after the beep.

Zeke quickly hung up his device and sent Miami a quick text:

"Please tell Kemi to contact me when you speak with her."

Zeke then immediately tried to reach Autumn.

You have reached a number that has been disconnected or is no longer in service.

His thumb hit the "end call" button quickly. Everything had happened so fast. *Who did this to my sister and Autumn?* Zeke wondered to himself while balling his right hand up into a fist and punched the palm of his left hand.

KNOCK, KNOCK, KNOCK!

"Zeke! Are you OK? I got you something to eat from Zaxby's!" said Mother.

"Thanks, Mom, because I'm starving."

As he stuffed his mouth with food, Zeke and his mother discussed all of the unwanted events that took place.

"I still can't believe that I was in a coma for two whole days!" Zeke said while eating a handful of crispy well-seasoned fries.

"Wow! Slow down. Don't choke yourself," said his mother.

"Hahaha!" he laughed while grabbing some water.

"I really wish... I knew who did this to them!" replied his mother as light tears rolled down her cheeks.

"Mom, it's just crazy because the whole time that I was in a coma, it was like I was there! There through all the pain, trauma, screams and cries!"

Zeke's mothers' eyes grew big as he told her his visions that he received while in the coma. She paced back and forth across the room without saying a word.

"Did you see who did this? And could you remember anyone's face?" she asked very impatiently.

"Everything was kinda blurred," he replied.

"Close your eyes and free your mind. I need you to focus," his mother said.

With his eyes closed, Zeke began to pull on all the energy that he felt from the universe. Right now, this wasn't such an easy task because all his strength was required, and he knew he had nothing really left. This would be a test to see how deep within Zeke's abilities really were.

Zeke thought to himself as he laid upon the bed helplessly. Images flashed and played in his head like he was watching a movie. At first, everything was blurry, but he continued to focus, and soon, everything became clear.

When Zeke opened his eyes, his mother asked, "What did you see, my son?" She became very worried from the expression on her child's face.

Armed henchmen with goat heads and pentagrams in the middle of their foreheads were all a part of Zeke's vision, and everything was pure evil.

"There were these demonic beasts," he said with lots of confusion in his eyes.

Rage filled Zeke's eyes and heart as the lights inside the small hospital room began to flicker on and off while different objects floated. Zeke's mother quickly touched his hand and said, "Calm down."

"Yes, son. Please calm down," said a familiar voice in Zeke's head.

The hospital door then swung open and it was like a thunderstorm inside the small room.

"Kim, let me speak with him for a second," said Zeke's father with lots of authority in his voice.

This has to be a dream, or maybe I'm still in a coma, because I haven't seen this man since I was 15. I'm 22 now! Zeke thought to himself.

Everything appeared to not make any sense at the present time. However, Zeke realized that he had to be alert of all things and stay focused. These visions were very extreme and valuable to him because they could contain the missing puzzle link that, perhaps, could mean something of need in the near future!

SEVEN-DAY VEGAN CHALLENGE

CHAPTER 6
A FLASHBACK TO THE PAST

Zeke and his family had moved to Atlanta in the year of 2001. His mother was tired of living in his father's shadow. Zeke didn't want to move from Brazil. He enjoyed the air and the beautiful Brazilian girl next door. Zeke had been crushing on her since grade school. He enjoyed the school he attended, plus the three-story house that sat perfectly on the beach, but things were getting real dangerous for his family in Brazil. It had been three years since Zeke last heard his father's voice. He was super excited when his father invited him to live in New York City. Zeke's father had left his past life alone and had made an honest living for himself. He worked his way into law school and became one of the richest lawyers in Manhattan.

"Absolutely not!" screamed Zeke's mother.

"Come on! Please!" Zeke begged.

"You don't even know who your father is! It's dangerous," she barked.

"Can't be as dangerous as those two vicious pit bulls that Alonzo has tied to the gate outside."

"He's right! Mom, just let him go!" Teresa interrupted.

"OK! But just for a month. Once I fill everything out, then I will make my final decision," said their mother while rolling her eyes.

"I hope that I don't regret this later!" she said to herself very self-consciously.

TWO DAYS LATER:

When Zeke exited the airplane, he was greeted by a limo driver who was standing in front of the airport and holding up a sign with his name on it.

"You must be Zeke. My name is Benjamin," said the limo driver. He opened Zeke's door and loaded his luggage into the limousine.

The ride through New York City made young Zeke's heart skip a couple of beats and his mind race a million miles an hour. This was his first time in New York.

45 MINUTES LATER:

When they arrived at a very tall building in the middle of Manhattan, Benjamin looked back and said, "OK, lil' Zeke. We are here."

His father lived in a high-rise on the 70th floor, so Benjamin helped him with all his luggage. When he walked inside his father's high-rise, it reminded him of something off *MTV Cribs*. Zeke's father was on his cellular device, and he was very well-dressed; the suit and Rolex watch he was wearing looked pretty expensive.

"Can you hold on one second, please?" his father said to the person on the phone. He turned to Zeke. "Hey, son. I'm glad you made it. I'm in a rush," he said while giving Zeke a tight, but brief, hug. "Listen, you are going to need some new clothes. I want you to have the best education, so you are going to a school of my choice, right here in Manhattan. Go put your stuff away. Benjamin will be back in the next hour to take you shopping. Here's my credit card. I will see you later." He got back on his cellular device and exited the high-rise.

I'm about to live it up in Manhattan with my Pops! young Zeke thought to himself.

With Zeke's mom being a single parent, money had been rather tight since they moved to Atlanta. In the next second, a hot, beautiful Spanish woman came from around the corner. She was like a breath of fresh air and her smile looked like a million dollars. She was wearing an all-black fitted dress, with a pair of all-red Prada stilettos that matched her all-red Prada clutch. Her walk was fierce, and she was headed Zeke's way.

"Oh! You must be Zeke. Hello! My name is Miranda. Let's have a brief chat because I'm late for a press meeting. If you think you're going to live here and steal my spotlight, then think again," she said while giving Zeke a huge smile.

When she walked out the front door, she slammed it with such force that the big, beautiful mirror that once hung perfectly on the wall fell to the ground and shattered into many pieces. Miranda quickly opened the front door and said. "You little badass. I can't believe you just broke that beautiful mirror. It costs more than the house your mother lives in. Now, clean it up! Ohhh, I can't wait to tell your father about this!" she said.

"I—I—I—I—I..." Zeke stuttered.

"Save it for someone who cares!" she yelled in a strong Spanish accent, then slammed the front door again.

"Oh, so, the devil *does* wear Prada. What's this woman's problem? She must not know who she's playing with. I'm not cleaning shit up!" young Zeke said to himself.

ONE HOUR LATER:

The limousine driver, Benjamin, had arrived and taken Zeke all around Manhattan. His father's credit card was on the verge of being maxed out at this point.

"What's wrong with you, lil' Zeke? Cheer up. You are the son of one of the most eligible bachelors in Manhattan," said Benjamin with lots of enthusiasm.

"It's my stepmother. She's a..."

"Whoa, whoa, whoa! Lil' man, your stepmother is a very powerful woman. Just give her a chance," said Benjamin with a serious Kool-Aid smile.

"Can we pull over to that store? I see a mink coat that I want."

The mink coat was priced at $25,000, but the sales associate gave the young man a huge discount. Benjamin took Zeke to all the hottest stores and filled his belly with some of the finest foods that New York City offered. Zeke didn't know how popular his father was until his name was mentioned in very exquisite and prestigious places. Zeke was treated like royalty at every store and every restaurant he dined in that day. He felt like a prince, and every prince demanded red carpet treatment.

"Wow, young man. You've spent $50,000 today. Did your father give you a budget?" Benjamin asked while parking the all-black limousine in front of the high-rise, which Zeke's father owned.

The young man had shopping bags from every major designer in town. Benjamin had to make five extra trips just to unload it all.

"Well, that's everything, young prince! Here's my card. Please call me whenever you need me," Benjamin said while handing Zeke his credentials. He looked inside. "Why is the living room covered in all that glass?" he asked with a look of concern on his face.

"I'm going to take care of it. Thank you, once again," Zeke said while closing the front door.

He looked around inside his dad›s luxurious living room. The broken glass that was shattered all over the floor looked out of place.

"I guess... I should clean this mess up. I did just buy a kickass game system with crazy surround sound," Zeke said to himself while thinking of the best solution to pick up the thick, broken glass.

TWO HOURS LATER:

Young Zeke was in his bedroom laughing and enjoying his new game and surround system when his equilibrium was rudely interrupted by screaming and yelling.

"Zeke!!!! Get out here, and now!"

"Why are you screaming my name so loud, woman?" Zeke asked, wearing a pair of Cheeto-stained pajamas.

"Pack your stuff! I'm sending your ass back to Atlanta and you will return all that stuff!" said the angry Miranda.

"I'm not returning anything. My father gave me permission to buy this stuff. What you need to do is stop yelling at me like you're crazy!!!"
"Nobody told your ungrateful ass to max that credit card out! You are in deep shit," said Miranda.

"I'm not going anywhere. This is my father's house and my father's money, which means it's my money, too."

"See, that's where you have it wrong. This is my house, and his money is *my* money. Now, pack your stuff. Your father will be here shortly, and we will be taking you back to the airport," said Miranda very sarcastically.

Slam!

Zeke didn't even let her finish talking. He slammed the door right in her face and locked it.

BOOM! BOOM! Bang! Bang!

"Open this door *now*! You don't slam doors around here!" yelled Miranda as she beat on the door like a rabid raccoon.

Zeke turned his new surround sound up so loud that it drowned her out. Story of the Year's "Anthem of Our Dying Day" filled the surround sound speakers as he listened to her bang on the door like a madwoman.

"Finally, the banging stopped," he said to himself while attempting to complete a mission on his game system.

FIVE HOURS LATER:

Knock, knock, knock!

"Son, open the door! We need to talk," said Mr. Banks.

Finally, my dad made it home! Zeke thought to himself with lots of excitement.

"Yo, what's up, Dad? Wait till you see this mink…"

Before he could finish his sentence, Mr. Banks interrupted and said, "Son... Miranda said you maxed out the credit card. Is that true?" he asked in disappointment.

"No, I spent…" Zeke tried to finish what he was saying, but was once again interrupted by the wicked witch.

"You are a liar, and you broke that big, beautiful mirror that was hanging on the wall!" said Miranda while she rolled her beautiful green eyes.

This woman is good, and she has my dad under her wicked spell. There's no telling what was about to take place next, Zeke thought.

"Dad, this trick is lying," Zeke said with lots of venom on his tongue.

"'Trick'?! Baby, he has to go," Miranda said while folding her arms.

"Zeke, you are just like your mother: rude and ungrateful. You are not about to come into my home and turn it upside down. I'm sending you back to Atlanta with your mother."

Zeke couldn't believe he had taken Miranda's side and his mouth dropped when this peculiar event took place. Miranda was standing behind Mr. Banks and sticking her tongue out, like a little ass kid, too tease Zeke! She looked more like a snake than anything else.

"Miranda and I are going to have dinner. We will be back in about an hour or so," said Mr. Banks.

Zeke's little feelings were beyond hurt, and his eyes burned because he was trying to hold back tears. His stomach felt like it was doing many backflips. His body went numb as he watched Miranda and his father walk out the front door.

Young Zeke's thoughts were everywhere. It felt like he was in the middle of a tsunami. He began to have devilish thoughts, the reason being was because he knew that this evil woman didn't want him around his own father. Miranda refused to allow anyone to take Mr. Banks's time from her.

Should I rip this house apart? Or maybe I should burn it down? thought young Zeke. As he packed his bags, the evil thoughts continued...

Beep! Beep! Beep!

A text message from his dad appeared on his cellular device:

Leave that stuff you bought. Don't pack any of it!

Even more rageful thoughts filled Zeke's spirit. Could such thoughts evolve from the cruelty that lay within his own heart pertaining to his father? Even though he was Zeke's father, he had no idea of the abilities that his son possessed! Or did he? Being the son of this man had brought more agony than clearance to young Zeke's life and current situation... which would lead him to perform more destructive behaviors!

Zeke walked into his father's room and began rambling through everything. When he opened his father's top drawer and moved a couple of items around, he found exactly what he needed...

BINGO!!!! There it was: Mr. Banks's checkbook, and also, another credit card. Next to it was $5,000 in cash money with a bank money clip on it. Zeke quickly reached into his pocket and called Benjamin. Moments later, Zeke arrived at the JFK airport.

"Good luck, young Zeke, and have a safe flight," said Benjamin.

A COUPLE OF HOURS LATER:

Zeke had landed at the Hartsfield International airport and, in a sense, he felt at peace.

"Finally, back in Atlanta," Zeke said.

Once he got off the train, he immediately caught a cab home. Zeke hadn't told his mother what had truly happened yet! He was waiting until he saw her face to face. Zeke's mother was waiting for him on the porch as she sipped on a nice, cold glass of white zinfandel wine. His little brothers, helped him unload his stuff. By the way, Zeke kept everything.

"Hahaha!" he laughed to himself very evilly.

While walking up the stairs, his mother said, "That didn't last long." Zeke gave her a quick smile and walked right past her.

"Son! What really happened in New York?" she asked as she sipped her wine slowly.

"Miranda didn't want me there! Hey, Mom, what can we do with this checkbook and credit card?" Zeke asked suspiciously.

"Just give it to me, son. I will handle it," his mother said with rage in her voice.

ONE MONTH LATER:

Ring! Ring!

"Hello?" Zeke's mom answered while putting the phone on speaker.

"Kim, I'm calling the damn police on you and Zeke. He stole my checkbook and one of my credit cards!" Miranda shouted.

"Yeah, yeah, yeah... Tell his father to call me. And are you really going to call the police on his son? Tell him happy birthday because you're on speaker phone. He *loves* the new SUV you bought him," his mother said with lots of sarcasm. "Zeke! Now, tell your father and Miranda thank you."

"Thanks, Dad," Zeke said while pulling into the parking lot of his favorite restaurant.

'Thanks' nothing... Keep the car and don't ever call me again in your life," his father said, then disconnected the phone.

That was the last time Zeke spoke with his father.

CHAPTER 7
THE PRESENT

FOUR MONTHS LATER:

When Zeke's Father walked inside the hospital room, they let bygones be bygones and came up with a solidified game plan to retaliate on whoever did this to Teresa and Autumn. Zeke's father also told him that he never sent a text message on the night he left New York City. So, the only other person who could have done something that devious was Miranda. He also informed Zeke that he stopped dealing with her after their third year together. Teresa was still in recovery. She also had undergone major plastic surgery and yet, she still needed more.

Well… Zeke still hadn't spoken with Autumn. It was like she left planet Earth, and this made him feel very uncomfortable. Kemi contacted Zeke and gave him the rundown on how Diego told her not to contact him anymore. Also, the prick told Zeke's best friend that he was wanted by the Feds and his phone could possibly be tapped. Now, what he failed to realize was that Kemi didn't care how much money he was spending on her. Her loyalty remained with Zeke.

SOMEWHERE IN MEXICO:

Keep the faith and know that all things work out for the greater good, only if you believe!

"Where is Kemi?" Zeke asked.

"She should be here any second now," Miami replied while swatting a small bug.

"How do you know that?" Zeke asked.

"I have my ways of knowing things," she replied while checking her social media websites.

Five minutes later, Akemi pulled up in an all-white Range Rover limousine. The limousine driver walked around and opened her door. When she stepped out of the luxury limousine, he grabbed her hand to make sure she had a safe exit. Akemi had on a big beach hat and an all-white Prada sundress that blew in the wind. Her hair was long and curly, with a Spanish wave that insinuated her Trinidadian features. Her gold-trimmed Prada sunglasses shone with each and every hit of the sunlight; you could tell she was being spoiled. Everything about her screamed "millionaire status." She met Zeke and Miami at a small restaurant less than a mile away from the beach in Cancun. The breeze and the view were impeccable. The waitress brought them out a round of Patrón shots and three big glasses of frozen Margaritas.

"OK, guys, Diego is back at the villa. The drugs I gave him should keep him knocked out for about three hours. He and Mr. Henderson have been planning something, and it's going to be big. They are highly intelligent, and they always speak in different languages that I can't follow."

"Do you think they are onto you?" Miami asked as she hit some of the finest cannabis that Mexico offered.

"Girl! I have Diego wrapped around my fingers. And did I mention that he even proposed to me? SEEEE?!" Akemi said while she showed them her engagement ring.

The only other engagement ring I saw that big was Mariah's! Zeke thought to himself.

Akemi pulled her glasses off, revealing her perfectly manicured skin. You could tell she was getting pampered; she even had gotten her teeth done, her makeup was red carpet ready and she represented true elegance and glamour.

Kemi slammed her hand on the table and said, "He did it, Zeke! He and Mr. Henderson sent them."

"How could you be so sure?" Miami asked while sipping on her frozen margarita.

"Because he talks in his sleep. Now, Diego and Mr. Henderson have lots of bodyguards..."

Zeke quickly cut Akemi off and said, "You just leave that to me. All I need you to do is enjoy the rest of your vacation. And also, while we are in Mexico, don't call me Zeke!"

"What do we call you?" Miami asked in suspicion.

Zeke chuckled. "Call me by the code name 'Money.'"

"Should we all get code names?" Akemi asked with lots of excitement in her voice.

"Girl! Just enjoy your vacation and make sure you go to the mall and grab a couple of souvenirs," Miami suggested while eating the fruit that hung on the side of her margarita glass.

"Let's take a shot for old times and one for victory," Said Money while they tapped shot glasses.

As the time slowly continued to pass by, Zeke and Miami figured they would have a little fun in Mexico, too!

Let the hunger games begin! Since we're all here, it might as well be our vacation! Miami thought to herself with an evil smirk.

While Akemi went to the mall and shopped a little, Miami snuck inside of her and Diego's villa. She walked inside and tiptoed to the bedroom where Diego was passed out cold.

"I wonder if he has some coins in here," Miami thought aloud, as she ransacked the suite. "Yes! Lady luck! Thank you! My favorite, Benjamin Franklin," Miami said while stuffing some hundred-dollar bills in her bra.

When she checked Diego's pulse, she gave him another dose of horse tranquilizer and laughed very seductively.

What no one knew was that Miami got a serious rush out of doing stuff like this. This is what she was born to do.

"Where is his cell phone? BINGO! I found it!" she said abruptly after rummaging through Diego's things.

Miami was a hacker, and she had her very own agenda. She quickly broke into his iPhone and also went through his photos and text messages, looking for anything that could incriminate him.

"Mmm! I see why Kemi was sprung," she said, then quickly focused on the task at hand.

"The tracker will only last for about three days, which will give me more than enough time to track all his locations," Miami said to herself as she smiled very evilly.

"Where the hell is Miami?" Money asked himself while he sat in the parking lot of the resort. "She was supposed to be in and out."

When Akemi's limo pulled up to the front of the resort, Money spotted Miami running from behind the building. She ran towards the car like Tina was running when she was trying to escape from Ike. She played it off well, though! "Hahahahaha!" she was laughing while holding her cell phone to her ear. When she entered the vehicle, a couple looked at her like she was a madwoman.

"Miami! Why did you just make that scene?!" Money asked while smoking a cannabis pre-roll filled with kush. She didn't give him any feedback. Instead, she flipped down the mirror, fixed her hair and re-applied her lipstick.

"AAAAAAHHHHHHHH!!!" screamed a crowd of people.

"What the hell, Miami?" Money asked in suspense. Loud fire alarms went off as all the hotel guests evacuated The resort.

"Just drive, Money! I couldn't hack into the hotel's computer system, so I triggered the sprinklers. It should damage the cameras and put a little water damage on Diego's phone," Miami replied, then snatched the pre-roll out of Money's mouth. He looked at her like she was crazy. "Haven't you ever heard of puff, then pass? Dang!" she said.

"Anyway! What's the point in that?!" Money asked while pulling out of the parking lot.

"You talking about the puff and pass or the sprinklers?" Miami asked with a stank face.

"Miami! Focus... I'm talking about the damn sprinklers."

"Why didn't you just say that? Anyway, Mr. Money, his screen is going to be blank for about 72 hours. The phone will still ring, though."

"Wow, you *are* smart. But also stupid, because how is Akemi going to get Diego out of the villa?" Money asked.

"Now, that's… something… I didn't think about..." she paused. "Oh, well! Akemi is a big girl, and she will figure it out. Hopefully the water will wake him up. It usually does," Miami said while shrugging her shoulders.

ONE DAY LATER:

Miami had flown back to Atlanta with Zeke; she was most definitely down for whatever and he appreciated her loyalty. You only stand on loyalty and respect!

"You know what? Miami, I need to introduce you to Yasmeen," Zeke said while turning the radio down in his brand-new, all-black, drop-top Benz.

"Money, please—I mean, Zeke. You're talking about Yasmeen with the green eyes? I know she is a contract killer. She and I don't see eye to eye! Ittt'sss.... kinda a long and complicated story!" said Miami while rolling her eyes.

Atlanta is so big, for it to also be so very small. There's no telling how Miami knew Yasmeen. All Zeke knew was that the girl sitting next to him was full of surprises.

"Anyway... what's the game plan?" she asked.

"Just lay low! Miami, you will see the fireworks very soon."

"OK, Zeke, check this out. I have to catch a flight to Japan tomorrow. You have my email; just contact me and I will be on the next flight to you. Bye, bye, doll face," Miami said while closing Zeke's door.

He watched as Miami exited his Mercedes. He admired her curves, her confidence and the vibes she delivered. It was almost as if she felt the energy from his eyes, because she quickly turned around and blew him a kiss like she knew he was watching her walk away.

"Damn! If this was a better time in my life, I would have been all over her. Where the hell are you, Autumn? If you can hear me, please give me a sign." A ladybug instantly flew on his steering wheel, and when that happened, he had an instant flashback. When Zeke and Autumn made sweet love all throughout the night, it was so powerful that the next morning when they woke up, the universe had covered their entire room with ladybugs.

"I'm glad you can still hear me! Love, I miss you dearly, as well. All we have in this world is our word, which means..." Autumn replied telepathically. Zeke made a promise that he would make whoever pay for what they did to Autumn and Teresa. For the rest of the way, his thoughts were pertaining to the avenging of his most sweet and beloved one.

CHAPTER 8
THE GIRL ON FIRE

MEANWHILE, SOMEWHERE IN BUCKHEAD, GEORGIA:

Miami had another agenda; she was not going to miss *any* of the action. Therefore, she decided to take matters into her own hands. As she followed Diego through the city of Buck head, he made a sudden left turn, then a sharp right turn.

Diego, I have a tracker on you. There is no need to turn down every street you turn on! Miami thought to herself while laughing and pulling inside of a local coffee shop.

Miami's IQ was extremely high, and in her line of work, she was one of the best. She already had a cab waiting for her just in case Diego tried something slick.

"Make a left, sir," Miami Instructed the cab driver while she tracked Diego.

FIVE MINUTES LATER:

The cab driver pulled into the parking lot of Phipps Plaza and when Miami exited the cab, she was in super agent mode. She had on a long tan trench coat with nothing under it. She was also wearing some big black Dolce and

Gabbana sunglasses with an all-black Carmen San Diego hat to match. She also had on an all-black pair of red bottoms that complemented her long ponytail. While she walked through the shopping center, Miami spotted a Face by Francois store.

"Well... while I'm here, I could use the new, top-of-the-line face care products."

"Welcome to Face by Francois," the nice lady at the door said.

"Can I help you with anything in particular?" Just'n said as he approached Miami.

"Wait, aren't you a news reporter?" Miami asked in confusion.

"Yes! You got me, my dear! I'm also the founder and owner of Face by Francois! Let me give you a piece of advice. It does matter how rich and famous you may become; never forget where you came from and never let anyone have total control over your assets! Never overlook someone because you may think they're not a worthy opponent. Always make the proper and necessary time to come by and check in on your establishments.

"Now, follow me. I have just the products that will get that face glowing in no time," said Just'n. "Our motto is, 'We aren't in it for the smell; we are in it for the look.' But I have a very important press meeting to attend. One of those young ladies will finish assisting you my dear," said Just'n as he exited the store. *Ummm! That young lady's face looks very familiar, and I never forget anyone's face*, thought Just'n as his driver opened the door.

"Where to, Boss?" asked the driver.

"Check your device! The entire itinerary is there!" Just'n said as the air suddenly changed.

"Don't move!" Two mysterious gentlemen said as they entered the all-black SUV.

"What is this, really?" Just'n asked with an unbothered attitude.

"Did you know that I have shooters all over this place! So, I would recommend that y'all don't do anything stupid!" Just'n said.

"Oh, yeah? You had shooters, but we took a couple of them out, and what we *do* know is that your SUV is bulletproof, so there won't be any bullets piercing this SUV! Now, driver, let's go on a little drive," said the mysterious man wearing all black.

"What is it that you need?" Just'n asked sarcastically.

"We need you to report that CIA Agent Samantha has been found dead."

"That's impossible! I can't report false news," said Just'n.

"You *can* and you *will*," said the tall English gentleman as he attempted to put his gun to Just'n's head.

"Hey! Wait. We didn't come here to harm Just'n," said the tall Spanish gentlemen, also dressed in all black.

"Well, what did you two come here for?" asked Just'n very boldly.

"We came here to cash you out," said the Spanish gentleman.

"And if I refuse?" Just'n asked while filling up a glass with some very expensive champagne.

"We will make you an offer that you can't refuse. Here, let me show you!" The English gentleman wrote everything down on a piece of paper and handed it to Just'n.

When Just'n looked at the piece off paper, his eyes grew extremely big! The note read:

We are offering you $100 million to report that Samantha's body has been recovered from the old warehouse.

"Gentlemen, your offer is very generous, but that's not my field or my line of work," said Just'n dismissively.

The two gentlemen were about to blow Just'n's top back, but surprisingly, Just'n remained calm through it all.

Screech!

The sounds came from the tires making a forced complete stop! The dust from the ground and the sudden friction from the brakes caused a weird mixture, which produced a cloud of grey smoke. Just'n SUV was now surrounded by 17 unmarked, all-black SUVs!

"What the hell is happening?!" yelled the Spanish gentleman as he attempted to look out the window.

Boom! Boom!

Blood spattered all over Just'n's very expensive suit as he sent both of the gentlemen to meet their creators.

"You fucked with the wrong one!" Just'n said very smoothly while cleaning blood from his face.

"Mr. Francois, are you OK?!" screamed an army of gentlemen as they opened every door of the SUV.

"I'm fine. Now, get me a clean suit! I'm now late for my press meeting," Just'n said as he pushed the English man's bloody corpse out of the SUV onto the dusty streets.

"Clean this up, and finish the driver, too! Thank you for my panic button that lays perfectly under my champagne glass," Just'n commanded his army. "I knew that would come in handy one day," he said to himself as he called his assistant.

"Please let my associates know that I'm running late and I will be there shortly!"

"Yes, Mr. Francois," the assistant responded as she sipped her green tea slowly.

BACK INSIDE THE MALL:
Mother Oshun

"The flawless face scrub will remove all those dead skin cells. The all-natural SPF moisturizing oil is not just for the face. You can also use it for your lips and hair. The toner is mixed with rosewater and it works wonders. I use it as a facial mist," said the African-American woman behind the counter.

"I will take the whole set, and I will take a Face by Francois T-shirt in small. I have to represent my flawless face once I'm finished," said Miami with a face of satisfaction.

"Sure thing! And thank you for shopping with Face by Francois," said the saleswoman, as she handed Miami her bag and receipt.

"Now that I've satisfied my shopping appetite, let me get back to business," Miami said to herself.

When she scanned the shopping center, she spotted Diego at the food court, and what she saw made her mouth drop. She immediately began to snap pictures.

"I knew he was a liar," Miami said, while pulling her cellular device out of her purse to call Akemi. "Giiirrrlll!!! You are *not* going to believe this. Drop your son off with his grandmother. You *need* to be on the next flight to Atlanta," Miami demanded.

On the other end, Akemi looked at the cell phone with a very confused face. She wanted to ask Miami lots of questions, but there was so much drama going on that all she could do was say, "I'll be there in the next five hours."

"I'll be waiting, girl, and please hurry!" said the determined Miami.

"Uggghhh… Girl, don't rush me! You know how I hate being rushed," said Akemi while hanging the phone up in Miami's face. *I don't know what all this is about, but I hate being dragged into all this drama,* she thought.

Maybe I should call Diego and let him know that I'm on the way to Atlanta. Akemi looked down at her beautiful diamond ring and kissed it with passion. *Naw... I will just surprise him,* Akemi thought to herself as she reapplied her makeup. When she got done, she packed herself and her son, little Dominic, a small travel bag, and they were on their way to Grandma's house.

FIVE HOURS LATER:
Forgiveness Is Key!

Akemi arrived at the Harts field International airport in Atlanta with a since of perplexed anxiety. She was confused and worried at the same time. She knew something wasn't right. Miami was waiting for her in an all-white Mercedes MLK. When Akemi exited the airport, Miami hit a small button to open the trunk. While Akemi loaded her Louis Vuitton suitcase inside the SUV, Miami was in the mirror putting on her lipstick. She quickly turned the radio up when Kemi entered the SUV and Destiny's Child filled the speakers: *If I don't pick up the phone like I used to for you, don't you take it personal!*

"Who are you about to break up with?" Akemi asked with a very confused look on her face.

"I›m not about to break up with anyone. Let›s go to Spondivits and eat some of the best seafood that money can buy in Atlanta!" Miami suggested.

"I heard about that restaurant and I've always wanted to eat there," replied the hungry Akemi.

"One of these famous rappers made a song about it, and it's only around the corner in Hapeville," Miami said while putting the Mercedes MLK in drive.

"Hello! Welcome to Spondivits. Can I take your orders?" asked a beautiful blonde woman.

Miami ordered for herself and Akemi. When the beautiful waitress was done taking their orders, she let them know that the food would be done shortly. "OK, Miami, what is all this about?" Akemi asked impatiently. The waitress came back with their drinks and placed them on the table.

"Thank you," Akemi said as she took back a shot of Patrón.

Miami sipped on her frozen margarita, and when she felt a buzz, she said, "Listen, girl…"

Suddenly, she was interrupted by the sounds of her ringing cell phone.

She looked at the screen, rolled her eyes and pressed the "end call" button. Miami pulled a manila envelope out of her purse and threw it on the table. Akemi's eyes grew extremely big.

"What is this?" Akemi asked with a face of confusion.

"Please stop with all the questions and just open the envelope!" Miami said with lots of anticipation in her voice.

When Akemi picked the envelope up off the table, Miami sat back and watched it all unfold. Akemi reached inside the envelope and pulled out a few photographs, and as she flipped through them, tears began to roll down her cheeks. She looked at each and every photo and felt dumb, hurt, used and betrayed. Miami quickly called the waitress over and told her to bring out another round of shots.

"How could he lie to me?" Akemi asked while she stared into outer space.

At this particular moment in time, Akemi's emotional state was not in the right place, because if she had a gun, she would have blown her own brains out! Even though she was loyal to Zeke, Akemi had been blinded by the fame and glamour that all of Diego's scams offered. The millionaire lifestyle that Diego introduced her to had poisoned her mind.

"I can't believe that I almost sold my best friend out. I was really going to marry this guy," Akemi said in shame.

Akemi›s heart had gotten involved with Diego somewhere down the line, and now, all she felt at that moment was pain. Raging thoughts crossed her mind as her heart turned ice-cold. All of Akemi's hidden demons had entered her soul at once and she was now out for blood. She felt nothing but hatred towards Diego.

As her eyes turned completely black, Miami yelled, "AKEMI!!! Snap out of it, girl!"

Akemi shook her head from left to right and broke down in tears. Miami immediately rushed to her side to comfort her.

"Miami, I'm lost for words," Akemi said while taking back two shots of Tequila and staring at the fish tank to the left of her.

"Listen, Akemi. I have an idea. The food is coming; let's eat. And here, girl, let's take another shot," Miami said while she took a shot, as well.

Miami hated seeing her best friend in tears. She watched as the strong and bold Akemi, who she always looked up to, broke down in tears.

"Damn. I wish I could call Zeke, but his head is not all the way clear, either."

"Diego has fucked with the wrong bitch! I'm about to rip his heart out his fucking chest!" Miami said to herself very rage-fully.

CHAPTER 9
DIEGO'S DESTRUCTION

7 HOURS AND 57 MINUTES LATER:
God judges humanity by the measure of their hearts!

Akemi and Miami had rented an all-black Tahoe SUV and they had been following Diego's wife, Khloe. He had been lying to Akemi the whole time. Secretly, he went behind Akemi's back and got married to the mother of his kids. "Miami, I just can't believe this. Girl, we've had several talks about this. He told me that he had no personal dealings with her. He told me the only time they communicated was when it was pertaining to his kids," Akemi said while she fixed her sunglasses.

"Well girl, he played too many games. Make a right and then make a left turn at Pleasant Hill Road."

"Miami, that's not where she's going."

"Akemi! I'm a pro. You never trail them. And besides, we have her address. Let's just park a couple of miles down the road from her house, and then we'll foot it! That way, there will be no trace of anyone's vehicle being seen at her house. We will catch her by surprise."

"Miami, you need to stop watching all these television shows. You are making me feel like you are living this life for real," Akemi said very suspiciously. Miami let out a slight giggle and then instructed Akemi to park the SUV.

Miami and Akemi changed their outfits to a pair of sneakers, biker shorts, a sports bra, a sun visor, a fanny pack and a pair of sunglasses each, with both wearing their hair pulled back in a nice ponytail. The two of them almost looked like twins. As Akemi and Miami jogged down the road, a car sped past them and honked the horn twice.

"Well, there goes our first honk. We must look hella sexy in our outfits," said Akemi.

The whole scene was refreshing for the both of them, especially for Akemi. Her mind, body and soul needed this jog; it allowed her to escape reality for just a brief moment. The summer breeze felt good against her golden skin, which cooled her down. She felt the pavement beneath her feet as she began to have flashes of Diego. She felt the burn inside of her stomach, which forced her to pick up the pace. She had forgotten that they were jogging; the lies, hurt and deception that Diego had put into the universe had taken over her. She took over the road like a lioness on the hunt for food.

"Slow down, girl!" Miami yelled.

MEANWHILE, INSIDE DIEGO'S HOUSE:

Khloe had just walked through her front door, and on her way upstairs, she reached inside her purse and grabbed four photos. As she sat on her and Diego's bed, she smiled and put the photos to her chest. Khloe was finally getting the life she always wanted. Diego had finally put a ring on her finger. She had been through hell and back over the years.

"Thank you, God! You have finally answered all my prayers. Now my children can have both of their parents in the same happy home," Khloe said to herself while letting out a giggle. Her thoughts were suddenly interrupted by the sounds of her cellular device!

RRRIIINNNNGGG!

She quickly reached into her purse and answered it. "Hey, Hubby," she answered as her face glowed and love filled her heart.

"What's good, Mrs. First Lady?"

"Oh, my gosh! You are so silly! Listen, I have some great news. Please hurry home," said Khloe with lots of enthusiasm.

"I will be there in the next hour," said Diego.

"I love you so, so much," said Khloe with a smile of seduction written on her face.

"I love you, too," he replied while exiting another woman's house.

Once she hung the phone up, she fell back onto the bed and let out a deep breath. Khloe pulled the photos even closer to her chest. I'm going to cook his favorite meal, put on some sexy lingerie and run his bathwater. She reached in the bottom drawer of the nightstand and said, "I can't forget about the candles."

Ding, dong!

The sound of the doorbell interrupted her thoughts. She dropped the pictures on the bed and ran downstairs to see who it was. Khloe was so excited that she'd forgotten the number one rule of the house.

"Who is it?" Khloe asked.

"It's your neighbors," replied the people on the other side of the door.

Khloe peeked through the peephole and unlocked the front door.

"Hi! My name is Amy, and this is Brittany. We are putting together a club for women." Amy pulled a flyer out of her fanny pack and handed it to Khloe.

"It's all about girl power. We are trying to motivate women around the world to stay in shape. Our slogan is, 'Yes, you can!'" said Brittany while pumping her fist in the air.

"You ladies look hot. Please come in. How long have you guys run today?" Khloe asked while taking a seat on her couch.

"We have been running for about 30 minutes," Brittany replied with a welcoming smile.

"Please have a seat. Can I get you ladies anything to drink?" Khloe asked.

"No! That wouldn't be necessary," Amy said.

"This looks great. How do I join? My husband wants me to get involved with things like this. I love your ring. You are a lucky lady, because, whoever paid for that ring, they spent a lot of money. You know what? I seen a ring just like that one in Puerto Rico, but my husband got me a better one," said Khloe while flashing her $2.3-million black diamond ring."

"The man is no longer lucky. He is now my ex," said Brittany.

"I'm sorry to hear that," Khloe said while putting her hand over her chest in concern.

"No! I'm sorry to hear *you*," said Brittany in a sarcastic manner.

Khloe had a serious, confused look on her face, and suddenly, the atmosphere in the room changed. Khloe got a real bad vibe.

"Oh, my God!!! Who did I just let into my house? Diego always told me to never let anyone in unless I called him first," Khloe said to herself in a panic. Amy pulled a small .22 handgun out of her fanny pack and pointed it at Khloe's head. "Don't open your mouth or I will blow your brains out!" she said.

In the next second, Amy pulled out a piece of paper and instructed Khloe to write everything she said. Khloe opened her mouth to ask a question and without warning, Amy shoved the .22 down her throat so hard that it chipped Khloe's beautiful front teeth.

"If you let out another peep, I will send you to meet your maker! Now, *write!*" yelled Amy."

When Khloe picked up the pen that Amy handed her, tears formed in her eyes, but she held them back. "Every word I say, copy it down," demanded Amy.

"Dear Hubby, you are a liar and you have played with my heart and emotions long enough."

Khloe looked up at Amy with such pleading eyes because she was so lost. She figured that if she was going to die, why not hear the truth? She wanted to know what was going on and why all this was happening. What had her husband done now? These are all the thoughts that went through Khloe's head.

SMACK!

Out of nowhere, Brittany slapped Khloe in the face with her pistol and said, "Now, write, bitch. We don't have time to waste or games to play!" Khloe picked the pen back up and continued to write the letter.

"Your other life has caught up with you, and now, my blood is on your hands."

As Khloe was signing the letter, her hands began to shake.

"Use this lipstick and kiss the letter," Amy demanded while laughing very evilly.

Khloe began to choke while she reached under the sofa to grab an all-gold nine-millimeter.

BOOM! BOOM!

Before she could even reach for the gun that was under the couch, Amy put two slugs into her chest.

BOOM!

"What the fuck, Brittany?!" asked Amy with a look of confusion.

"She was moving," Brittany replied with a devilish grin.

Amy shrugged her shoulders and said, "Oh, well! the dumb trick should›ve just let the poison on the lipstick work. Let›s go, girl." She headed towards the front door.

BOOM! BOOM! BOOM!

Brittany sent three more slugs into Khloe's head… well, what was left of it. Blood and brains were all over the living room. The pretty, all-white polar Bear fur that covered the living room floor was stained for life. Khloe's blood continued to leak as her body released all of its waste and fluids.

"Let this be a message to your husband. Save a spot for him, because he is next!" said Brittany, with lots of satisfaction within the tone of her voice.

Amy then grabbed Brittney and the both of them ran out the house.

Five Minutes Later:
The Seals Have Been Broken, But Which Seal Are We Living In?

Amy and Brittney hopped in the Tahoe they had parked down the street and quickly changed out of the clothes that they were in.

"Brittney, girl, I meant Akemi. Why did you put so many bullet holes into that woman?" Miami asked with a voice of concern.

Nevertheless, Akemi didn›t say one word. She just continued looking straight ahead.

All she knew was that she just murdered someone. She had just taken a woman's life and thought she'd feel bad afterwards and didn't. Strangely, it actually felt good.

"Miami, I believe that I'm a natural-born killer because I feel good on the inside! I have a lot of adrenaline pumping through my veins right now!" Akemi said with the biggest smile she had given in a long time.

"Honey, because you did 'a good deed,' that bastard came for your family. He caused you pain and brought you a headache! So, now it's time for his heart to break. Girl, karma is a bad mother..."

"Shut your mouth," Akemi said to Miami while she put the SUV in drive. Then they both drove away into the wandering night.

Back at Diego's House:
Follow the Principles of Ma'at!

"Khloe! I'm home! KHHHLLLOOOEEE!" Diego stopped in his tracks and his feet went numb instantly as his sight rested on what it captured. His body went completely limp as the roses in his left hand fell to the ground. Diego fell to his knees and tried to reach for his pistol that was inside his gun holster. As hard as he tried, he couldn't, because Khloe's blood was everywhere. His beloved, Khloe's, brains were splattered all over the living room—all on the walls, the furniture and the floor. He knew it was her because of the butterfly tattoo on her right thigh. He mustered up the strength to stand while reaching for his gun. This time, he was successful!!! Diego started running through the house like a madman in hopes that he would find the intruders or catch them in action.

He ran upstairs to their bedroom and walked over to the bed that Khloe once slept in. He picked up the ultrasound photos off the bed and his heart dropped...

"This is what she wanted to tell me. She was pregnant."

Diego didn't know how to feel at the moment. He ran back downstairs in search of clues. He looked at his wife... well, what was left of her. While he looked at his once beautiful wife, he had many flashbacks of all the drama, pain and heartbreak he took her through over the many years. All he could do was look up to the 30-foot ceiling and say, "I'm sorry baby, for all that I took you through over the years."

Suddenly, his spirit led him to look down at the coffee table and there it was: a mysterious letter from Khloe and it read:

Dear Hubby,

I love you so much and my feelings for you will always be the same, but you are a liar and you have played with my heart and emotions long enough. Your other life has caught up with you and now... my blood is on your hands.
Love Always,
Khloe
Muah XoXo

Diego was beyond hurt! Angry tears filled his eyes while his heart turned even darker. If there was any light left in him, it had just been snuffed out by the current situation!

He knew that all of this chaos was his fault. Khloe's death was because of him, but who did this? *I've done so much dirt in my lifetime… Now, my wife and unborn child are dead!* he thought to himself.

"What am I going to tell my two other kids?" Diego asked himself aloud while holding the bloody letter.

"Fuck, Khloe!!! I told you to never open the door. Why didn't you call me like you always did? Damn, baby. Who did this to you?" Diego asked the mutilated corpse of Khloe.

While he paced back and forth, sweat ran off his face like he was a man who had been working out all day. «Whoever did this to you will pay," said the angry Diego as he got onto his knees and hugged Khloe›s dead corpse.

CHAPTER 10
ZEKE'S BATTLE WITHIN THE BELLY OF THE BEAST

One Day Later:
The Horseman That Brings War Has Arrived!
Has the Antichrist Taken Over?

"Hey, Teresa. I bought you some new flowers and you still look beautiful. Carlya and Maurice are doing just fine. You are going to beat this!" said Zeke as tears began to roll down his face.

Teresa laid on the hospital bed and wasn't even responsive to the slightest touch. The doctors had her under some serious medication. She was healing fast, yet she had more work that needed to be done.

"I love you, bro," said the unresponsive Teresa in a very dry tone of voice.

This is the first time I've heard Teresa speak. This gave Zeke a great sense of peace, but at the same time, rage and pain filled his heart.

"Get better, sis… You just wait until…"

To Zeke's surprise, he was suddenly interrupted by the injured Teresa grabbing his right hand…

"It's already done, bro. You will have your time to shine… Just be patient," she said, using telepathic waves.

I can't be crazy… Why haven't I noticed any of these signs? Teresa has the gift, too, but how has she been hiding it from me this long? Zeke asked himself as he kissed her on the forehead.

This could only mean one thing. Teresa has a gift and her abilities are stronger in areas than mine! Zeke thought to himself. He quickly grabbed the keys to his Benz off the small table and exited the hospital room.

He had some unfinished business to take care of.

Akemi and Miami had to get out of town. They both went their separate ways; Akemi flew back to Florida and Miami flew to Japan.

For what, though? Only God knows the secrets that lie within the belly of the mysterious Miami. What Akemi didn't know was that Miami had hired private protection to watch over Akemi and her son until she returned to the States.

In spite of all the childhood disagreements they've had and all the things they've experienced, the girls treated each other as if they were blood sisters. To hurt one of these beautiful ladies would be signing you and your family's death warrants!

Inside Teresa's House: A Horseman Named Death Is Upon Us All!

As Zeke laid back on Teresa's living room couch, he tried to clear his head because it was so cloudy. His mother tried to smooth things over before she left, a few minutes ago, but deep down inside, he knew this was far from over.

BEEP! BEEP! BEEP!

Zeke looked down at his cellular device and It was booming. He had 15 missed calls and four new text messages. Message number one was from his sister in law, Shuga Shayna. She was scheduled to marry Zeke's older brother, Alonzo, in the near future.

Message number two was from his other mom,, who was a very powerful and wise woman:

Hey! Don't forget to chant: Namu Myōhō Renge Kyō! Love you.

Message number three was from a famous dancer and choreographer, and also the husband of the beautiful and talented star. He worked with many famous artists.

Message number four was from Ramirez Williams, CEO of 3P Entertainment, who was also a formal member of Choppa City Records.

Message number five was from Kia inviting Zeke to an spiritual meeting. Zeke was booked for several photoshoots, and a business associate wanted him to fly to LA for a video shoot. He quickly powered off his cellular device because he needed this time to himself to put the missing puzzle pieces together. As he laid back onto the sofa, all he could do was think about Autumn.

LOVE ALWAYS WINS:

HERE TELLS A STORY ABOUT AN ENTITY, WHO ONCE GOT THEIR HEART BROKEN AND VOWED TO NEVER ALLOW THAT TO HAPPEN AGAIN!

CHAPTER 11
THE SEVEN TRUMPETS!

"If you don't untie me…!" Samantha demanded.

"You don't call the shots around here!" Paris replied with lots of vengeance in her voice.

"300 million more to go. Then, we will think about keeping you alive," said Kay as she smoked her pineapple vape.

"You will never get away with any of this!" Samantha barked.

"Please put something in her mouth to shut her up. I can't concentrate," said Paris while moving the money that Samantha stole from them.

"You're all dead!" Samantha yelled right before Fatima stuffed her mouth full of dirty socks then duct taped them shut.

"You are one nasty, ruthless bitch!" Tokyo said.

"Girl, ain't that what y'all call me for?! Hahaha," Fatima chuckled as she flipped her long, perfectly dirty blonde hair very seductively.

Inside The US Embassy, North Tower:
Another Horseman Has Arrived! Death, Diseases And Plagues Follow Them. They Will Destroy One Third of Earth's Population.

Agent Dixon sat inside his new office. He received the big promotion that Samantha had promised. Dixon was not an unjust man. The new promotion, office, pay raise and perks weren't satisfying to him because all of it was built on

Samantha's lies. Dixon tried several times to reveal what really happened, but everyone in the north precinct just thought he was just being his usual humble self. Even though Dixon was pissed that Samantha shot him, he knew exactly why she did it! He couldn't drop the case; he knew Samantha was still alive somewhere. Dixon sat at his desk and watched the video footage that he recorded at the warehouse. His mind continued to race because he knew there was an unsolved mystery here.

"Maybe I should turn this footage in to my superiors," said Chief CIA Agent Dixon.

Dixon hadn't turned Samantha's operation in yet because he needed more information. Dixon battled with this case and wanted to find out if Samantha was alive or not because if she was truly dead, then Operation Mongoose would be buried with her.

Dixon reached inside of his drawer and pulled out the case file, which read:

Mongoose.

He began to receive a massive headache because the evidence that he had on Samantha would be so major that it would hit every major news and radio station. The money and recognition that he could receive would be off the charts.

SLAM!

Dixon slammed and locked the file inside his drawer right before his assistant walked in with his morning coffee.

"Hello! Good morning, Chief," said his assistant while handing him a cup of hot, fresh coffee.

Her fresh perfume pulled him away from the stress that he was feeling! When Dixon looked her in the eyes, he saw the most beautiful woman in the world. His manhood began to rise in his perfectly tailored suit pants.

"Oh! Chief, is this a bad time?" said his assistant as her insides oozed.

"No! This is a perfect time!" Dixon said while adjusting his manhood.

"I have the case files you requested," she said very nervously.

"Did I make you uncomfortable?" Dixon asked her with shame in his voice.

"No! No!" she said as she fanned herself.

"So, you are my new assistant?"

"Guilty as charged," she replied with a cheerful smile.

"You look familiar! What's your name?" Dixon asked with an eye of suspicion.

The woman was very attractive. Hell, she was absolutely stunning! Her beauty was out of this world. Her outer beauty wasn't the overall picture; it was her inner beauty that Dixon admired. She wore a pair of clear-framed designer glasses and her pencil skirt insinuated her natural curves. She was about five feet, six inches tall and her natural golden skin shined like the sun. Her smile was brighter than the moon and her hair was pulled back in a nice, full bun. Her bangs touched her eyebrows, which brought out her honey brown eyes. The new assistant had nice, full, juicy lips, which was driving Dixon crazy.

"My name is Paris… Paris Winters!" she stuttered as she watched his manhood grow.

"I'm sorry. This is really embarrassing," Dixon said while turning around to face his desk.

"No! It's not embarrassing!" Paris said as she admired his full chocolate skin and his unique physique. The energy in the room was so hot that someone could cook a full-course meal within seconds.

Beads of sweat dripped down both of their bodies and it danced off their skin like disco balls that were beating to the rhythm of their hearts.

"Let's have lunch later," Dixon said, trying to soften the mood.

"I would love that. Is there anything else you need from me?" she said then bit her soft lips gently, which drove Dixon up the roof.

Dixon hesitated for a moment. He wanted nothing more than to bend her over on his desk, then flip her over while her red bottoms dangled in the air!

"Noooo… that's all for now!" he said in his strong Jamaican accent.

"Ahhhhhh," she moaned to herself as she walked out of the office very professionally.

"Whew! Who was that woman? She kinda looks like the girl from the warehouse! Maybe I need to take a vacation because I could be making assumptions," he said, then took a sip of the coffee that Paris delivered him.

When Paris walked out the office, her heart skipped many beats because she felt like she had found her soulmate. No other man had ever made her feel that way. The spiritual energy that was just projected in that room seconds ago had her feeling like she took five shots of the good shit; she was in pure, heavenly bliss. Her phone vibrated inside of her purse and when she looked at the screen, she was brought back to reality.

"Fuck, can a girl dream?" she said to herself while sliding into the women's bathroom to answer the call.

"Is it done?" Fatima asked.

"No! I need more time," said Paris with a face of irritation.

"I don't think you're the girl for the job," Fatima said sarcastically.

"Do you know what I had to do to get this Job?"

"Not too much of anything. We made all your documents and plugged you in," Fatima chuckled.

"You're right! Haha."

"Paris, do you have a slick crush on that agent?" Fatima asked with a voice of suspicion.

"Why do you say that?" Paris asked nervously.

"Girl! Kay and Tokyo told me how you were chosen at the old warehouse."

"I have work to do! I will call you later, Fatima," Paris said while quickly disconnecting the call.

Once Paris ended the call, she put the phone to her chest and walked out the bathroom stall to make sure she was the only one inside the bathroom." I'm not killing him, but I will continue to watch him closely," Paris said to herself, then walked out the bathroom with many different motives.

Back at a Secret Location:
A Pale Horse
Everything You Have Been Told On Earth Is a Lie! Reprogram Your Mind So That You Can Start Receiving the Proper Downloads!

"She just peed on herself," Fatima said with a look of disgust.

Smack!

Fatima quickly hit Samantha in the face with her pistol.

"Damn, girl!" Tokyo said, then sipped her lemonade while watching some anime.

"Somebody gotta have some type of order around here! Where is Kay?" Fatima asked with a face of confusion.

"She had a business meeting!" Tokyo said very dismissively.

I need to take matters into my own damn hands! Fatima thought very viciously.

Samantha looked around and she couldn't believe her life had turned into such a tragedy! "I'm so sorry, Autumn!" she said to herself.

The lack of food, water and rest really affected her brain. The urine that she was sitting in was sticking to her leg and it felt like the end of the world. Her head pounded from the bullet that punctured her temple! Ever since that tragic moment, Samantha felt different, almost like she had a wakeup call. Her heart was softer and she didn't have any more vicious thoughts. She just wanted to hug Autumn tightly and put some flowers on her dead husband's grave that she had abandoned over the many years. She wanted to free her workers, clear their names and get them off that horrible private island. She was even prepared to give them an even share of the cash they stole, and donate the rest to the Save the Children Foundation.

"I wonder how Agent Dixon is doing. If I ever make it out of here, I have to profess my love to him and let him know that the love that we made wasn't only just a fling! I wanted nothing more than nothing but to be Mrs. Dixon. He probably hates me! I was a monster to him. I really screwed up this time!" she said to herself while more regret filled her newfound loving heart.

"What did I miss?" Paris asked as she walked through the front door of the secret location!

"Nothing but little Miss Pissy Pants over here!" Fatima replied with a face of irritation.

"How was your lunch with your new boo? I mean, boss."

"Fatima, it was just lunch!" Paris replied as her face turned rosy.

"Details! Details!" Tokyo demanded very impatiently.

"You two have clearly been in here too long smelling Samantha's pissy fumes! It's getting to your brains. And besides, a lady never kisses and tells," Paris said jokingly.

"She's no fun," Tokyo said and then resumed her anime.

"It really smells like we should put her in the shower," said Paris while holding her nose.

"Girl, you do it. I'm not touching her, because if I get any closer to that bih, I will slit her throat! She took $9.2 million out of three of my accounts! This shit is real personal," Fatima said as she headed towards Samantha.

"Let me go, Tokyo!" Fatima yelled while holding her switchblade open.

"We are not gonna kill her just yet, Fatima! I will take care of this pissy mess!" Paris said abruptly.

"Fine! I'm late for a pedi and mani, anyway! I will see y'all later!" Fatima said. When she exited the safe house, she threw up the deuces and slammed the door.

"Tokyo, are you going to help me?"

"You on your own!" Tokyo replied while munching on a bag of chips.

"I will just call for backup!" Paris said as she pulled out her cellular device.

"What is the problem?" Miami asked.

"I will send everything via email," Paris said, ending the call.

Samantha looked at Paris and she couldn't understand why she had a badge from the US Embassy. *Did she turn me in? Or worse, maybe she's going to kill Agent Dixon! I wish I could warn him about her.*

"Is there a problem?" Paris asked Samantha while Samantha stared at Paris from head to toe.

"Do we have anything to temporarily put over her face?"

"Yes, we do. I can handle that," Tokyo replied while pausing her anime TV series.

Paris rolled her eyes and went to the other room to change out of her uniform. As Paris got undressed, she received a mysterious text from an unfamiliar number!

The text message read:

I had a great lunch. We need to do dinner. Only if you're not too busy! I just feel like we've met before and I love your spirit! You have really great energy.

Back at Chief Dixon's House:
432Hz…. That's the Love Frequency! Meditate On It Daily! The Apocalypse Is Upon Us All!

"I need the location of every private island that this Central Intelligence

Agency is aware of. Also, I need you to forward to me all Samantha's computer data that's in her office! *And* I need a copy of all her phone records," Dixon demanded as he chopped up some fresh vegetables.

"Paris really looks like the girl from that warehouse. I know I'm not losing it," he said, then took a sip of very expensive wine.

"Incoming text message from Paris," said his cellular device assistant.

"Read the text message," he said.

"5:35 p.m.: Hey! How are you? Dinner is confirmed! What's the location and what time?' Do you want to reply?" asked the cellular device assistant.

"Yes!"

"OK, what do you want to say?"

"Dinner at my place will be 8 p.m.! Wear something comfy."

"Message sent," said the cellular assistant.

Back at the Safe House:
There Are Very Few Pure Souls Left!!!

"He wants me to come to his house, which seems weird!" Paris said while she and Miami gave Samantha a shower.

"What's wrong with you, Paris? You're drowning her!" Miami said. Then, she quickly snatched the shower head out of Paris's hand.

"I'm sorry. My thoughts are everywhere!" Paris said.

"Anyway, she is clean enough. Do we keep her in these wet clothes?" Miami asked as she turned off the water hose.

"Please! I need fresh clothes!" said Samantha while she shivered and shook.

"Shut up!" yelled Miami and Paris.

Miami immediately stuffed the old socks back in Samantha's mouth and secured them with fresh duct tape. Paris wasn't present in the current moment because she couldn't take her mind off of Chief Dixon; she didn't know if she was about to walk into a complete ambush. Her mind, body and spirit were telling her otherwise.

A Rude Awakening:
Many Lost Souls Are Trying to Steal Your Very Essence!
Be Careful Who You Tie Your Soul With. It Can Become Detrimental for Your Well-Being!

"They did *what*!?" yelled Mr. Henderson.

"She is dead!" Diego cried very pathetically.

"Who's dead? Speak up, son!"

"Khloe. They killed her," said Diego as he paced back and forth through Mr. Henderson's house.

"Take a seat, because you're talking in gibberish," said Mr. Henderson while pouring the both of them a glass of bourbon. "Who killed Khloe?"

"Autumn and Zeke!" Diego said as he pulled out his pistol, then cocked the hammer back.

"Hahaha!" Mr. Henderson chuckled.

"What's so damn funny?"

"Foolish boy. Sit down and have a drink!" demanded Henderson.

Diego followed direct orders and had the drink Mr. Henderson just poured him. The warm bourbon burned his chest, but it eased his mind!

"Do you feel a little better?" Mr. Henderson asked with a grin.

"Why are you so calm and what do you know?" asked Diego with a face of confusion.

"Autumn and Zeke didn't kill her!"

"How can you be so sure?" Diego said as he flipped the chair he was sitting in. He paced around Henderson's office a little more.

"Because I had Autumn beat half to death! Zeke is losing his mind! And he is next. I have plans for him," said Henderson with a sarcastic tongue.

"Who do you think killed her?" Diego asked as he positioned the chair that he just flipped and took a seat.

Mr. Henderson knew Diego had lots of secrets and he was very unbothered by the situation at hand because he had bigger fish to fry!

"Let's have another drink. Then, we will figure this thing out together. And I highly recommend you get rid of that device in your back pocket," said Mr. Henderson with a nonchalant attitude.

Meanwhile, at Chief Dixon's House:
The Key to Eternity Reunites With Mother Gaia!
Another Horseman Has Arrived. This One Will Destroy All!

"I'm glad you could make it," said Dixon. He put a fork full of fresh steamed vegetables into his mouth.

"The food is delicious," said Paris.

"Let's cut to the chase! Who sent you?" Dixon asked with a stern face.

The air in Dixon's house suddenly changed and everything turned black and cold for the brokenhearted Paris. She didn't know what was about to come out of his month next. His eyes changed to a different color, and suddenly, he wasn't so transparent anymore.

"I'm confused!" she replied, then sipped on her wine.

"Don't worry. I will get the truth out of you shortly," he said with a sinister face.

Suddenly, Paris began to choke on her food and her throat felt strange. She tried to pretend that nothing was happening to her body, but what she failed to remember is that she was dealing with a Central Intelligence Officer!

"Were you at the warehouse on the night that my ex-partner, Samantha, got shot?" he asked, this time with a smirk on his face.

"Yes, I was."

"Very good! The truth serum that I put in your food is working!"

"You put *what* in my food?!" Paris yelled while attempting to leave the dinner table.

"Sit down! I have questions and you *will* answer them!" He yelled, then slammed his hands on the dinner table.

Paris instantly sat down. She was scared and turned on at the same time; she didn't know how to feel. Whatever he gave her had her feeling funny and she felt very vulnerable.

"Next question: Do you have feelings for me?"

"Yes! I actually think I'm in love with you!" she said with pleading eyes. His eyes grew extremely big because he had deep feelings for her, as well, but how can you have deep emotions for a person that you haven't even known for more than 48 hours. Nevertheless, he had to figure out who she was and what she actually wanted.

"Do you know where Samantha is?" he asked, then he took a sip of wine while staring her deeply into the eyes. *Damn, she is so beautiful. She almost looks like an innocent butterfly that needs my protection.* He quickly dismissed the thoughts and continued his interrogation.

"Yes, I know where Samantha is."

"Is she alive?" he asked.

"Yes, she is alive."

"Is she somewhere safe?" he asked.

"Yes, she is safe—for now!" Paris replied forcefully.

"Do you know that you could go to jail for a really long time, gal?!"

"Yeah, and so can you. I know that you haven't turned Samantha in, and that's withholding evidence during a serious federal investigation! It's your job to report your findings and you haven't! So, let's face it. If I go down today, you will, too, and Samantha won't make it out alive. Plus, her little operation will be all over every major news station, radio…"

"OK! I get it!" Dixon quickly interrupted.

Paris watched as the tables turned. She was now in control of the situation, but she wanted to rip her clothes off. The truth serum had her not only telling him the truth, but she was now able to live in her own truth! Paris got up, walked behind him and gave him a soft, gentle hug. He then let their hands touch for a brief moment right before he spun her around and looked passionately into her eyes. Their bodies collided and it felt like Mars just ran into Venus.

"Now, I have one final question!"

"I will tell you anything! Ahhhhhh!" she moaned. As their lips barely touched, it sent instant chills to her sweet flower!

"Did someone send you here to kill me?" Dixon asked while he brushed her left nipple aggressively with his right thumb!

"Yes. I was sent here to kill you, but I never had any intention of doing it. I just wanted to meet you. From the moment I saw you at the old warehouse, I had fallen for you!" Paris replied.

Tears rushed down her face like a stormy night! He felt the lightning within her soul, and it felt like the battle of the bands. He listened to the rhythms of her pulse, and he knew everything she said was true! Dixon still had lost all trust for her.

"I don't trust you! But I want to trust you and I want to love you! So, how about we just start all over with a new clean slate?" he asked as he held her tightly.

"I would love that," Paris said while his manhood pulsated against her stomach.

"Let's finish dinner and you can tell me all about yourself. Then, we can figure out what to do about Samantha together."

"I'm down, and you're such a gentleman," said Paris as he pulled out her chair.

"You are welcome. Now, let's eat!"

The Safe House:
The Ancient Ones Will Restore Order:

"Where is Paris? And has the lady eaten?" Miami asked with frustration within the tone of her voice.

"I don't know where Paris is, and Kay hasn't returned, either!" Tokyo said, dismissing the other question pertaining to Samantha's well-being!

"Well, I have something to take care of. I'm not a babysitter, yet it seems like I'm babysitting you and her," Miami said right before she walked out and slammed the front door behind her.

"Now, the *real* fun begins!" Tokyo said with a sinister tone. She pulled out a blowtorch from under the bed.

Samantha's eyes grew extremely big because she didn't know what the mysterious and mischievous Tokyo had planned!

"No! No! No! Please don't!" She attempted to scream, but the duct tape blocked that out! She didn't know what was about to truly take place as Tokyo headed her way with the blowtorch.

Meanwhile, Inside Miami's SUV:

"What the hell just happened? How did I just lose Diego's trail?" Miami asked herself while hitting the steering wheel.

"Please leave your…"

Click!

Miami immediately hung up with a frustrated heart.

"Why is Zeke not answering the damn phone?! I may have to call Yasmeen! She may be the only person who still has a little sense left because it seems like the world has lost their damn minds completely," she said, then turned onto the highway.

"Yasmeen speaking! I knew you would have to come back home to Mama. You miss me, don't you?"

"You play too much," Miami barked.

"Come meet me in Russia and wear something sexy! I've missed those lips."

"I've missed you, too, babe," said Miami as she rubbed her flower! Hearing Yasmeen's voice had her insides flooding while her clit thumped!

"I will send you the location where one of my private jets is. Everything will already be set for you. See you soon, my love."

When Miami ended the call, she couldn't believe that it went that easy! "I better still be ready for war when I see Yasmeen," she said as she headed to the airstrip.

CHAPTER 12
WHERE IS LORD ENKI?

Teresa's House:
The Phoenix Has Risen!

Zeke's thoughts were suddenly interrupted by loud banging that was coming from the front door...

BANG! BANG! BOOM! BOOM!

"Open up! It's the U.S. Marshals!!!"

Zeke's heart began to beat uncontrollably fast as he searched for an escape route.

"Damn, what do I do? Think, Zeke, think..."

He peeped through the blinds and they had his sister's house surrounded. 15 all-black unmarked SUVs sat outside along with a couple of military hummers. "Open the door or we'll kick it in! We know you are in there!" yelled A U.S. marshal!!!

"You don't know shit. Y'all all say that same bullshit!" Zeke yelled to himself as he continued to panic.

He quickly looked up and pulled the string to the attic. He then climbed the ladder, and once he was inside, Zeke closed the attic door and found a safe spot where he could hide.

BOOOOOM!

"What in the hell? They just kicked the door in!"

RUFF, RUFF!

"*And* they brought the K-9 unit for me. Who do they think I am, Bin Laden or something?" Zeke asked himself as he sat in the hot and itchy attic.

When he looked down at his cell phone, it disappointed his heart because he should have never turned it off. His dreadlocks were extremely long, and they were getting in his way, so he quickly pulled them back and tied them up into a knot. His armpits began to sweat and drip; the summer heat mixed with the stuffy and dusty attic had him ready to turn his own damn self in.

Sssqqquuueeeaaakkk!

"They just opened the attic door. God, please help me! Let them just go about their business!" he prayed, in hopes that the Alpha and Omega would hear his humble cries.

"If you don't come down, we will send the dogs up!" another marshal yelled!

"How in the hell did they know I was up here? Well, there's nowhere for me to run!" said Zeke with defeat in his soul. "No, no, no… I'm on the way down. No need to send the dogs up!" he yelled with some sense!.

When he climbed down the ladder, several officers had their guns drawn on the 22-year-old. Three K-9s barked very loudly and were ready to shred the 140-pound Zeke into pieces!!!

" Put your hands behind your back!" yelled a marshal.

When Zeke was being carried away in the back of the police car, his thoughts and spiritual energy were out of balance. He knew that one day, this life of schemes and scams would catch up with him. It was all a reflection of his childhood.

The Past:
(Tasting Blood for the First Time)

Zeke looked around at the house he lived in. It was big, but not big enough.

He was hungry and thirsty—and not for food, but for money. He had always been too smart for his own damn good and way too grown for his own age; that's what many older people told him. As he walked through the hallway, he noticed that his mother's bedroom door was wide open. He quickly peeked inside to see if everything was OK; it appeared to him that his mother was stressed to the max, to the point of no return. Whatever was bothering her, it had to be serious.

But knowing my mom, she's a very strong woman, young Zeke thought. Nobody would ever know what she was actually going through, because she never put her weight on other people's shoulders. Sitting on her bed, she scanned through many bills, and the natural hustler inside young Zeke had the gears turning within him!

"I know we're not still living off the duffle bag that was full of money from years ago. How much was really in that bag?" he asked himself.

Zeke never told anyone what he witnessed that day. He had always kept his mother's secrets to himself.

"If she were to go to jail, it would be her own self to send her, not me," said Zeke, not even knowing he had just cursed his own life.

The tongue speaks life and death. Always be mindful of what comes out of your mouth because it can bless you or curse you.

As he tried to creep past her, she asked, "Zeke, where are you going?" "Outside for a walk," he replied.

Her facial structure changed and she said, "Outside for a walk?" with such aggression!!!

It was like those words were telling her that I've just shot my teacher in school or something! Zeke thought to himself while attempting to exit the house. Mother gave him a stern look that could cut through steel. Then, she went back to looking at those damn bills again. He already knew what his mission was. His hands were itching extremely badly because he needed some cash and he *knew* he was about to get some cash!

A celebrity who's in a girl group lives in our neighborhood! But where? he asked himself.

I know that I can get some cash out of her purse! Zeke thought to himself as he continued to walk through the huge subdivision.

The summer heat was hotter than the kitchen at Grandma's on Thanksgiving night.

He continued walking down the street and froze in his own tracks when he saw a very beautiful woman who appeared to be in distress. From the look on her face, it appeared that something terrible had happened to her.

So, Zeke stopped to see if she could use a helping hand. There was nothing wrong with her; she was just having a man problem. She was talking to Zeke like he was old enough to understand anything she was saying. The only thing on the young man's mind was the green.

I've heard enough of this woman!!! Now, give me the cash right now! he thought to himself as he continued to listen and look at her with a nice, big smile full of deceit.

Even the poor little dog in her hands was tired of all the shenanigans, so the little fellow jumped out of her arms. She then began to panic while screaming to the top of her lungs. Zeke quickly ran after the little doggie.

When he approached the dog, she jumped into his arms. Zeke then took the little fellow back to its owner.

"Oh, my! Thank you!" the lady said very dramatically.

"You're welcome, ma'am. Hey, can I ask you a question?"

"Sure! What is it?" the lady replied.

"Do you know any famous singers who live out here?"

"That would be me," she said with a cherry smile.

"BINGO!" Zeke quickly shot her his sales pitch and she went for it. At the end of their conversation, the beautiful lady reached into her purse and gave him a nice $100 bill.

MY BESTIE, MY BEST FRIEND

Zeke was in love with money. It was like a drug to him. He couldn't explain the rush or high that he got, but what he *could* tell you was that he was hooked for life. The celebrity woman was one of his victims today.

Thanks for the cash, he thought to himself as he smiled evilly.

He hit twenty more houses that day and his pockets were sitting on 22s. While walking down the street, he wondered in suspense. He wanted to know how much money he had actually made!

" I need to stop and calculate how much cash I have on me," said young Zeke as he reached inside his pocket.

He pulled out a piece of paper that had the lady's autograph on it. "I will keep it close because it will be worth millions one day. I really am a big fan, but being a fan doesn't put food on the table at the end of the day," he said.

From that day on, he knew he was destined for greatness with his famous girlfriend by his side, and not to forget running into the famous singer that day. He had just found one of the missing puzzle pieces to his life.

Slam!
Get Ready for Chow Call!!!

His thoughts were interrupted by the nasty guard slamming his cell door. While sitting there staring at these four walls, he thought to himself. He just couldn't believe that he was inside this rat hole. He just went from eating caviar to slop. Looking to his right, a famous rapper was at the door, rapping and beating on the fours walls, trying to create a beat to keep his flow going…

He was a very powerful, talented, and misunderstood artist with great poetic potential and a serious head for business. He made lots of mistakes, but who hasn't? We live and we learn to grow from all of our past mistakes. Life is funny sometimes… oh, wait. That's too cliché. You know what makes life funny? Sometimes, we simply don't understand it. If knowledge is power, then what is power to knowledge? Let me tell you…. it's understanding—that's what you have to establish. Remember, life is what the Creator gave you for free. However, *style* is what we do with our lives. You must deal with yourself as a worthy individual and make everyone else deal with you the same way.

Zeke pulled the covers over his head and just prayed that he could just go to sleep, then wake up; that this nightmare would vanish and his life would resume back to normal, but this is what happens in… Atlanta!

In a city full of money, sex, drugs, lies and murder...

What happened to Samantha? Will she survive in the hands of the mysterious and mischievous Tokyo? Will the love affair between Miami and Yasmeen turn into a beautiful love story, or a beautiful, bloody bath?

"What do Diego and Mr. Henderson have planned for Zeke? And did they play a part in his sudden run-ins with the police?

"Will Diego find out who really killed Khloe?"

"Will Agent Dixon and Paris's bittersweet love story last?"

"What happened to Autumn, and will she ever be found again?"

"What lies beneath the mysterious and powerful Just'n? And what did Samantha do to him? Why does he want to track her down so badly?"

"Who is Zeke?"

"Why did Kay suddenly disappear? And will Dream and Brandon live a safe and normal life? Or will Henderson's goons track them down?"

"What will happen with Akemi? And will Teresa ever make it out of the hospital?"

TO BE CONTINUED.

CHAPTER 1
A COLD-BLOODED KILLER

In the beginning, God created the heavens and the Earth. He also created goddesses and gods as well. However, somewhere going towards the end of humanity, Zeke was born in the Dominican Republic and his family didn't like the fact that his mom had a baby outside of their race... well, their bloodline. His mother ran inside the house sweating and breathing heavily, grabbing everything that she could.

"Teresa! Teresa!!!" Mother yelled for Zeke's big sister. She and mother were like night and day. Mother quickly grabbed three nine-millimeters and put two in her purse and one in Teresa's hand.

"You remember how to use this, right?" Mother asked with aggression in the tone of her voice.

Teresa pulled the hammer back and said, "You're damn right."

Mother wanted to whip her ass for cursing, but she quickly brushed her thoughts away and said, "Good girl. Now, run upstairs and grab your brothers."

Teresa then stuffed the gun inside her little pink purse and took off running. She stopped all movement when she heard Mother screaming her name. "Yes, Mother?" Teresa replied very calmly.

"If you see anybody you don't know, blow their fuckin' brains out," Mother said as she pulled the floorboard up.

What no one knew was that Mama had some serious cash hidden throughout the house.

Teresa nodded her head and ran upstairs to pack up some clothes, then met Mother downstairs, where she was pacing the floor back and forth while peeking out the window in a sneaky way.

"Mom, are you OK? And where are we going?" Tony, Zeke's older brother, asked while sipping on a cold soda.

"To your father's house," she replied.

Teresa knew something wasn't right. At ten years old, she held that nine-millimeter so close and tight inside her little pink purse. The little girl was ready for war. While the family was heading to the carport, an all-black SUV pulled up and their mother's intuition immediately kicked in.

"Get back!" she yelled.

BOOM! BOOM!

Mother quickly looked back in shock while her heart raced a million miles.

"What?" Teresa asked. "You said, if I see someone I don't know…"

The little ten-year-old had put two slugs into the head of the man driving the black SUV.

BOOM! BOOM! BOOM

Mother finished the job by shooting at the gas tank, sending the SUV and whomever was in it to cloud nine. The distraught family ran around to the back of the house and Mother pulled the cover off of an old, rusty pickup truck that had a nice boat attached to it. The family watched in silence as their mother put fire to their house.

On the drive, gospel music filled the speakers of the old pickup truck. Mother always tried to make the very best out of any situation. She always had a bright and passionate sense of humor. Mother and Teresa began cracking funny jokes, trying to soften the mood on the unexpected journey. 20 minutes later, the family was being loaded onto the boat that was once attached to the old, rusty pick-up truck.

Mother ran back and put something inside the gas tank of the old truck.

As the family rode off into the coast, they all heard a loud BOOM! and watched as the old pickup truck went up into smoke and flames. On the boat ride, Teresa asked the million-dollar question.

"What is going on?"

"Your uncle robbed the damn cartel," replied their determined mother.

TO BE CONTINUED.

Volume 1:

The Beginning

www.ingramcontent.com/pod-product-compliance
Lightning Source LLC
Chambersburg PA
CBHW050450110726
47899CB00003B/880